Other Books of Poetry by Jeff Reed

In Search of J. Morton Allen (2015)

Volume One:
Collected Poems and Other Writings (2013)

Estuarial (2013)

Less Than City (2012)

Mene Tekel (2012)

A Penny for Your Thoughts:
Poems to Bouguereau's Young Girls (2011)

The Song of Christ (2009)

Waking Up in Wales (2008)

The Ascension Window (2008)

The Cast (2008)

Available from Wind in the Reeds Publishing at:
www.lulu.com/spotlight/windinthereeds

Kóre

on the Trail of the

Tree Keepers

---

by

Jeff Reed

Wind in the Reeds Publishing
Walnut Creek, California

PUBLISHING

Copyright ©2015 by Wind in the Reeds Publishing
1141 Bont Lane
Walnut Creek, CA 94596

Windinthereeds.tumblr.com
windinthereedspub@gmail.com

First Edition – September 1, 2015

Cover Picture by Bess Hamiti, Podujeve, Kosovo
Used under the Creative Commons CC0: Pixabay

For information about permission to reproduce selections
from this book, write to:

Jeff Reed
1942 Alvina Drive
Pleasant Hill, CA 94523

ISBN: 978-0-9897389-6-5

Acknowledgement

I am indebted to Dr. Peter Kreeft and his wonderful book *Back to Virtue* (Ignatius Press, 1992) in which I first encountered the brilliant notion of contrasting the traditional seven deadly sins with the Beatitudes of Jesus. For this structural device and for many accompanying insights that have found their way into this work, I am most grateful.

Dedicated to
John Reed
a man who has lived a life of virtue

Contents

ONE:

ESCAPE

———————

The red-boiled sky faded at the edges
of the world, the estuary of dusk
trickling coolness down upon the chase,
relentless since the sun had shaken day
awake to witness what had then begun
to unfold at a tense terror-soaked pace.
Queen Jezebel on horse-drawn chariot
with fifteen soldiers and a pack of hounds
hunting with a vehemence her prey—
young courageous Kóre on the run
with her owl companion, Yeoman (as
she had named him on the day she found
the owlet tangled in a spiny broom).

Kóre, dark-haired, feisty, full of life,
though skin and bones could give a gang
of boys their match in fight and tongue and wit,
preferred over these the company
of gentle creatures of land, lake, and sky.
Yeoman, still an adolescent Eagle
Owl, could spread his wings a full five feet,
his orange eyes set beneath two pointed
tufts like the brows of a wise professor.
And wise he was. Pure-bred nobility
marked his character: loyal and most
affectionate. No truer friend could Kóre
ever hope to find, and most glad now
that she had found him before this troubled day.

13

Half-crazed dogs salivated at each scent
of Kóre's bread-crumb path with every drop
of blood from blistered feet and battered knees.
Sweat and filaments too fine to see
proved a treasure map for the keen-nose dogs
self-suffocating in their vigorous press
against their neck ropes and the whitened knuckles
of the handlers dragging on behind.
Always in the air above the party,
like a foul and lingering witch's mist,
curled Jezebel's cursing voice in whine
scratching sky and ear with plaintive vow:
Whether canyon, creek bed, distant border,
Kóre, every refuge sought will fail!
You belong to me by family order,
witnessed by great Asherah and Baal.

On this night pass there would be no moonlight,
as it is before the waxing crescent.
Present only stars, and even then,
for all their number the heavenly light was thin.
Kóre breathed her gratitude out slowly,
face an island, body submerged in
the dark gentle current of the Jordan,
drowning scent and carrying Kóre down
into the narrow canyon where the caves
would give her for the night a hideaway

far below the Queen's incessant rants
and the howling of the restless pack,
furious at the sudden loss of trail.
Yeoman had already cased a cave
(an expert scout on wing as owls can be)
where they would hole up and she eat crumbs
of bread, and he the spiders that would dare
traverse the cavern walls in search of prey
only to become it. So would pass
the first night eluding the clutch of the clammy
hand seeking to drag Kóre into
her lair and there devour her dignity.
Seven days before, her father Naboth
had been stoned to death on false pretense,
a trumped up charge, a ruse to gain the rights
over Naboth's vineyard. Only child
Kóre, left to next of kin, became
a pawn of favors, subject of a pact
between her aunt and Ahab, greedy King,
promising Kóre as a lifetime slave
and a plaything for the Queen's desire,
bargained for a tired piece of land
then belonging to the royal house.
Yeoman, hidden in the shadowed arches,
witnessed the dark covenant and flew
warning Kóre who, without hesitation,
fled into the Wilderness of Zin.

A fitful sleep gave way to frightful morning.
The lightening sky, though placid, promised more
panic-fueled chase as in the distance
faint echoes of yelping dogs mixed with
the cheerier birdsong easily overpowering it.
Weighed down by exhaustion even before
rising to her feet, cold despair
breathed on Kóre's heart making it hard
to breathe, and she, unsure how long she would
be able to keep on running and evading
Jezebel's chariot, dog-and-death parade,
in downcast tone to Yeoman she spoke gravely:
Yeoman, let me lie here, let me die here.
Better death than feeding on this fear;
Better death than being found by her.
To be found by death is better far.

O my Lady, Yeoman said in turn,
(for he was a rare owl who could speak)
I know our predicament looks bleak.
This is how I felt caught in that tree
before you came around and rescued me.
You have ever since been a living sign
that what seems nigh impossible just might
be in fact around the coming corner.
Remember how the cup and bowl from clay,
soft and fragile, harden only after

prolonged heat? How the sweetest laughter
follows terrible trouble gone away?
Easy joy is shallow joy at best.
Deep joy seeps up through the darksome test.
Let us not succumb to devilish ploy.
I see yet a future filled with joy.

You speak true, with courage too, wise one.
Kóre's piercing green eyes brightened up.
Lead on, then, and I will keep my eyes on
what hope calls out from the far horizon.

The narrow canyon of their refuge lay
between two openings to the north and south,
where at both ends, eagerly standing guard,
the hunters waited to see in their net
Kóre tangled up upon exiting
the safety of the deep river ravine.
Jezebel commanded the long vigil
as it was she had all the time
in the world, while for Kóre time
was slipping like the grey-green river by.
Yeoman disappeared for half the day
and returned when sun was at its height
and heat was thronging all along the bluff
driving life into crevice and shade.

Suddenly into view from up above
dangled down a wondrously woven rope
of branch-skin from a grove of olive trees
nestled atop the cliffs on the high plateau.
Kóre was astonished at the sight.
Yeoman reappeared with laughing eyes
and said he'd found a flock of sunbirds there
ready to assist a plot to spoil
any desire of the hated Queen.
A thousand of them in concerted swarm
stripped the branches of their leathery bark,
wound the pieces length by length into
a rope long enough to reach the bottom!
Kóre then with Yeoman on her back,
flapping wings to power her upward climb,
hand over hand scaled the sheer cliff wall
feet on stone and held by olive tether
to the top unnoticed by the hounds
and hunters busy staring at the mouths
far away at either canyon end.
Deep into the wilderness they fled,
step by step and second by second widening
the spread between them and the dark pursuers,
who continued glued above their traps,
transfixed by the cadence of the Queen:
Fair I have you, fair I own you! Mine!
There is no where left to run and hide.
Kóre, come out. Yet I might be kind.
Leave illusion of escape behind.

Without stopping, without looking back,
Yeoman in the air above and Kóre
on her bruised feet hustled into evening's
welcome. Cooler air and deeper shadows
coaxed them further in the Wilderness
of Zin on an ancient dormant trail
they happened on quite by providence.
Far enough away now from the hounds
to use a trail and easier for the feet,
Kóre followed along its winding route
until around a bend it split in two
at the base of a gnarled Juniper tree.
There she fell to rest among its roots,
forming as they did a kind of bed.
Yeoman brought her water from a stream
nearby. Down they settled for the night,
wondering what the morning light should show,
two paths offering opposite ways to go.

TWO:

ELIJAH,
KEEPER OF THE JUNIPER AT RAVEN'S CROSSING

The leathery weathered trunk twisted upward
like a cyclone long ago frozen
in mid-whirl beneath black desert clouds.
Its streaked grey bark lay in petrified wraps
around the stem of a stalk of wild-hair green,
bunches of needle-leaves bushy at the head
and hiding in its cage the home of a Keeper.
Kóre in the morning awoke to the loud
and animated greeting of Elijah,
Keeper of the Juniper at Raven's Crossing.
His head poked out from a cluster of leaves
like an odd and ill-timed blossom insistent
on being born. He scrambled down and
sat in the S-curve of the Juniper's twisted trunk.
His warm way from the high tree dispelled
alarm, and Yeoman fluttered up to rest
beside the ancient prophet, jovially content
to break his morning chores upon the sight
of the unexpected gift of company.
His bold nose well protruded from between
the bush of salty beard and wild brow.
His faded garments held by leather belt
smelled of smoke from burnt mesquite.
Dancing eyes and a deep-rich voice charmed
the morning stillness into dance and hope.
Kóre told him of their plight and he
in turn with somber tones turned serious
and set about the setting things in clear

concerning her dire predicament:

Being chased by evil or to find it
ever crouching in dark shade ahead,
waiting as a leaf-buried net tight-spread
across your path, must always be in mind. It
is life, and not that God designed it,
but leaving room gave evil fertile bed,
and it is now the air. Eden's dead.
The choking Cherubim-dust has been unkind. It
must be noted though, you have advantage;
in your case the evil has a name
and echoing noise that easily tracks her antics.
Jezebel is obvious and this will play
to your favor since you know her game,
allowing you to always avoid her way.

Note the smell of evil. Sickly sweet,
like a fruit left too long in the sun,
all its natural goodness overrun
by rot of excess, gluttony of heat.
What in seed is good, when grown, defeats
its native goodness when it dares become
other than design's prescriptive sum,
and so begins to run on foreign feet
to foreign places merging alien
allegiances until the first is lost,
and last of all, unrecognizable,
trapped within itself, it can't begin

unraveling the amalgam that is full
of spoilage from the line long crossed.

Be aware that evil dons disguise.
Its favorite is the raiment of the light
and cloaks behind the motive that seems right,
expert in its bent to rationalize.
Every evil has a root that lies
in what was at first good and pure and bright
for God made nothing evil in His sight.
But every good thing can be bent, where dies
the good and in its place with equal power
and potential is released the poison
to work its bidding in the later hours,
brewed in shadow and shade into illusion,
steering if possible the pure in heart
toward swallowing the smallest seed of dark.

Time there is to fight and time to flee.
Fleeing is not cowardice, but wise
when strength seems upon the enemy's side.
Fools will fight to prove temerity.
Make the stand on your terms. Such will be
when you have a cavalry close beside.
Now is the time to run. And I will guide
you toward the haven of your destiny.
To the left: Mt. Horeb. Going right
will wind you back the way that you have been.
Seek the stone-circled mountain, blackened top

and awe-inspiring, where the Queen will stop
pursuit for she is dread to come in sight
of that holy mountain's smoldering rim.

Kóre found Elijah's cadence peace,
and confidence she drew in from his gaze.
Wishing she could linger longer there,
she hesitated to rise to her feet.
But Yeoman dropping down from higher perch
snapped her back to the urgency of the hour.
From the tree Elijah dropped a bundle
of fine angel cakes baked in the sun
and a jar of water, one he said
would refill each night of its own accord
as long as she not dip it in any pool
or stream along the way. She placed the gifts
into the pack she wore upon her back.
And so in generous spirit the friends bade
each other warm farewells and to the left
the owl and girl took their trail with speed.
The sun was in the open of the sky
juddering the horizon line apart.
And way off in the distance, if they stopped
to take a drink from the water jar or eat,
by listening hard, the faintest yip of dogs
plagued the breeze with the hint of coming foul.
And sounded time to time, whether wind or true,
a low-moan voice of *Kóre, Kóre, come!*
to which the fugitives shook out their ears

and set their sights on Horeb with resolve.

The way wound up and weaved among large boulders
strewn about by some celestial collision
long ago, when lesser moons were vying
for the honored circuit now held by
Luna that we know, which was visible
in the pale blue sky, though afternoon
had not yet run its course with evening waiting
in the wings. On wings Yeoman circled
above the hillside, surveying twists and turns.
Kóre kept rehearsing in her mind
Elijah's hard words gently handed over.
With all her might she set intention toward
reaching Horeb's slope in forty days
as he had done so long ago, and she
would find the Cave where the whisper reigned
in place of fire and quake and ripping wind.
There she and Yeoman would make home,
if the Mighty King of Horeb allowed,
of course, and she would live her grateful days
as abbess of the Cave giving care
to pilgrims fleeing from the violence of
the raping world, for such was she now
and should she be delivered she would give
away to others that which she'd been given.

The boulders began giving way to brush,
then bush, then larger bush, then smaller tree,
to taller trees, and now a kind of forest,
casting shadows' long lines as the sun
dallied on the horizon as if he
were hesitant to give in to the pull
coming from beneath the jagged line
where land kissed sky (or sky kissed land). The trail
here was slightly overgrown, sheltered
as it was from heat, but still it led
on steadily. Long since had been
another traveler wandering through this grove,
all the ground cover thick and undisturbed.
The way remained discernible and so
led the fugitives up toward a bluff
overlooking a narrow wooded vale.
Beside the trail a long neglected sign—
forged, in its appearance, by a primal
people, intricate and showing off
a marvelous craftsmanship of skill and eye,
smothered now by ivy and the slow
fade of glory beneath the beat
of uncompassionate time which cares not for
the preservation of neither body nor art—
faithfully bore its message in a script
that somehow Kóre, not knowing how, could read:
Warning! All who dare travel beyond
this point! And here the words in smaller print
put forth explanation: *Be it noted*

that a numinous air flows through this valley
which origin lies deep in Horeb's mines.
To breathe this charmed air once is to be changed
unalterably in blood and brain and bone.
While it makes one fit for Horeb's climes
it renders a return impossible
back to all the desert lands from which
this trail has led the traveler to this sign.
Before it is too late muse on this fact:
to proceed means never going back.

Kóre wondered deeply at these words.
She had never once considered this
flight from Jezebel a final exit
from the lands and people of her birth.
But what choice now did she in fact have?
Behind her on the trail gaining ground
was slavery or death, synonyms
in her mind. Horeb lay ahead
and required a special constitution,
which in truth, if the sign be true,
sounded like improvement. *Let us,*
Yeoman, onward into Horeb's track!
Kóre cried out with her fist upraised!
To the plough, hands, and no looking back!
Life ahead! To risk this is no fault!
To falter now is pillory of salt!
Yeoman fluttering full of approval
led the way over the crest and down.

Into the wooded valley they descended
noticing at once the cool sweet air
swirling all around them though not one
leaf on nearby bush or tree was stirring.
The smell was unfamiliar but something
like a fruit. One could almost taste
the viscous lusciousness thick in the air.
And coolness too. But not in simple drop
of temperature. Coolness like a soothing
rag on the forehead of a fevered brow.
Coolness like the calm of quiet sleep
on the burning heels of a harried day.
A deep-down freshness petal-like when dew
dangles on the lip before the drop,
splash and scent inextricably linked.
Kóre at the first swirls felt lightheaded
and her field of vision blurred for a moment or two,
like in the twisting of the telescope lens
before the crystallizing clarity
of the focused aim. Everything
around her took on depth and dimension:
crisp line edges set layers in relief.
Shadow and shade kept to different realms.
Colors leapt out as if suddenly freed
to show themselves to the world as they were.
The white patch atop Yeoman's head now
looked gloriously like a mountain
cap crowned with snow. And Yeoman
wondered to himself if ever before

he had seen such green as Kóre's eyes.
The crickets now began to raise their strums,
and evening breeze stirred up the voice of trees
as sounds too joined the chorus of distinction.
If one listened each strain could be well
distinguished from the general mash of noise:
the distant birdsong *cheevio-chee* and *pirit-*
pirit played in counterpoint, and not
competition, *tswuh-tswuh-roo* and the *coo*.
The wind above the trees played lighter strains
than the wind that combed the middle way.
Even the crunching of the twigs and stones
beneath Kóre's feet as they walked along
took on such an appealing tone, as if
the very earth was playing percussion in
the orchestra of the twilight wooing night.
Thus in a spirit of calm and soul-delight
the two companions slowly wound their way
on the breezy wooded path, down, up,
down, up, and finally to the other
crest of the far-side rise and then onward
along a flatter plain but plush with leaves
still, and though the cool sweet breezes swirled
no longer, everything now was different.
A friendlier star-flocked night sky like a wrap
held the moment in an elegance
that for a short while dimmed the memory of
the deadly chase that had brought them here.
It was several hours later when the moon

was at its circuit's proudest pinnacle
that the path dead-ended at a fork wherein,
at the intersecting point, there stood
a tree, immense, with thick branches full,
a great Terebinth the height of a tower,
its trunk like a pillar holding up
the moon. Yeoman, now on Kóre's shoulder,
looking left, then right, spoke what both
of them were thinking in light of the puzzle:
Without a sign to tell us which is Horeb's
way, I rather think that we should wait
the night out in the shadows of this covering.
We need some sleep as the hour has grown late.
The mulch leaf beds were soft. The water cool
from Elijah's jar, now nearly empty
from the day's long journey. Nearby ran
a stream and Kóre thought to fill the jar
with the tempting water but remembered
that to do so would drain out the magic
of the jar. She could wait till morning
to see what mystery would manifest
while they slept. The angel cakes were sweet
and in the abiding of that manna taste
she fell into the merciful space of sleep.

THREE

ABSALOM,
KEEPER OF THE TANGLING TEREBINTH

Little did they know that they had come
upon the famous Terebinth of old
which had caught up Absalom by his hair
and foiled his plot to take his father's throne.
Hanging still, although his hair had grown,
Absalom, Keeper of the Tangling
Terebinth, looked down upon the travelers,
glad to see companions come his way,
for lonely is the life of one forever
tied by irreversible knots to branches
of a stubborn tree. But he would see
the cause and purpose of their night time visit
in the morning light when his "hullo"
would be kinder and less a terrible start.
With the morning birdsong, buoyant light,
and smell of ripened berries in the sun,
Absalom called out to greet his guests:

Hail there, strangers! Wake to a promising day!
I am so glad that you have come my way
for I am in sore need of company!
Wake and tell me why you've come this deep
into Ephraim's Forest. I can see
that you have already passed Elijah's tree.

Kóre startled awake, and Yeoman too,
who flew between the girl and the dangling man
(who had let himself down by his hair

hanging just above them now), so strange
it was to be bolted wide awake
by an air-borne hair-suspended man.
But moments only to assess that he
whose face was pained was kind, and who could not
harm them if he wanted, seeing he
was held within the boundary of his hair's
length. And so Kóre told the tale
of Jezebel and their narrow escape
from the Jordan canyon and their sweet
visit with Elijah and the passage
(she glanced down at the jar to see it full!)
through the valley where the air of Horeb
had filled their lungs and changed their eyes and ears,
and now their quest to make the arduous trek
to the safety of Mt. Horeb's Cave,
and how this fork had stymied them at night
as they were wondering which way led them right.
Absalom, Keeper of the Tangling
Terebinth, cheerily gave them aid.
This is an important junction indeed.
Providence encouraged you to wait
so that you could know what lies ahead
on either branch of the trail that divides here.
Pointing to the left way he began:

On this path you will soon wend
to the high Plateau of Pride which stretches wide,
a distance which seems to lengthen side to side

36

the faster one pursues toward either end;
where one grows smaller, swallowed up within
the span of its vast space until one's stride,
though frantic, no advance is verified,
and motion is to stillness as a twin.
And as particulars grow indistinct
the features of one's self become the sole
field of view with any clarity.
And so it comes as natural bred instinct
to lock one's look down at one's hands and feet
to hold on to some sense of something whole.

There the wishes of the boastful bloom
in fullest blossom, though few recognize
their earlier wishes, present but disguised,
as when the telescope on highest zoom
sees the rail but cannot see the room,
and how it is that all inflated size
erases wrinkles, but as surfaces rise,
bloating sweeps its path out like a broom,
distorts what's fine into a caricature,
magnified into a swelled grotesque
mockery of what it was before.
Once it was the arrogant were sure
that bigger would be better, more is best,
until they put the theory to the test.

There is only One able to bear
that kind of size though He will not insist

on dissuading those who will persist
upon the Plateau, and He will share
the weight of the divine and will not spare
the pressure that breaks Atlas' bending wrists.
"Come, ye gods, who by free will enlist
to carry the world and breathe in all prayer,
exhale independence; take your place
among the burning stars and furthest gasp
of the cold vast corridors of space!
Stretch your skin to seize within your grasp
the sheet of worlds to shake! Now shake! Now shake!"
To unimagined thinness they awake.

At the same time, then, growing small
compared to the horizon, and expanding
compared to themselves, they run standing
still, becoming nothing, becoming all.
I know. It was on the Pride Plateau my fall
into ruin was realized. My base ranting
against my father's grace, his free granting
mercy where there clearly was no call
for it, was his weakness. Were it mine
to do, I would excel him on the throne.
So I stole allegiance by deceit,
and on the rooftop took his concubines,
drunk on dreams until abrupt defeat
left me hanging helpless and alone.

He paused within the sadness of the moment,
as once again on the wide walls of his mind
played the tragic story of his choice
that led to the spearing of his many dreams,
pierced and emptied, leaving only this,
their haunting replay reels with vividness
accessible at any time of day
to torture him with that which might have been.
Then with a start he steeled himself to take
the moment to redeem the past with this
opportunity to steer a stranger right:

To the right a valley you will find,
low and plain, and through which runs a stream
fed by subterranean springs, which seem
hardly worth the mere mentioning, blind
they'll be to travelers' eyes, hidden behind
surfaces. This fetid brook, though slow, is teeming
with life, and along the banks, the reeds lean
over the water casting cool and kind
shade where dragonflies and damselflies
thrive, frogs and salamanders alive
in their small worlds complete, content.
The Great Blue Heron side by side
with the Least Bittern, and the bent
world prospers well where the lowliest lies.

The way to Horeb winds along this brook
and into a marshy meadow where you'll sink

up to your knees in muck and mud and stink
until you cannot stand another look
at the wetland stretch that you mistook
time again for dry land, and you'll think
to come back here, to turn left and to link
with the High and Mighty Plateau in which no nook
or crevice sits insect-infested water.
Dry is the way of pride, clean but thin.
Mark my words and heed my warning, daughter!
Do not turn back but press on through the wading.
Looking boggish, with your tired hope fading,
you will finally find firm ground again.

The Poor-Spirit Bogland is a trial
that works a wonder in the deepest place
within us, ferreting out the slightest trace
of believing bogs are meant for others while
we are not meant for the bogs. You'll smile
at the other end, after grueling pace,
when you look in a mirror at your face
and see the grime and splash, what once so vile,
now looks human, takes on common air,
and fitting, in its clinging speckled way,
on you as it would be upon any,
to which if you can laugh, no longer care,
you'll find a source of strength for the many
remaining trials that on your journey await.

And here is the great secret it will teach:

forget yourself and you will find the wide
world full of space in which to run inside
it, not like the Plateau that shrinks your reach,
but rather bringing near to your hands each
beautiful "other" from which you need not hide,
but where your lack of defense will serve as guide
into its world, creature meeting creature
with respect and undiminished conviction.
Days will pass and you will realize
you haven't thought about yourself and called
in comparison. No compensating disguise
forced to duty in a quick conscription.
Living free, and living free with all.

Absalom grew silent. Kóre knew
he had told them what they needed to know.
Looking at the downward path she sighed,
imagining all the wet that lay ahead.
Only if she too had wings like Yeoman,
she could take to sky and so avoid
having to choose paths like now she must
between the dry Plateau and the marshy vale.
But owls must have their crossroads too, she thought,
though what they were she told herself to ask
Yeoman sometime down the trail. She drank
the water from the jar and felt renewed.
Preparing to set out, she reached to shake
the hand of Absalom, and when she did,
he placed in hers a comb and said to keep

it in her hair; it had the power to keep
her afloat should come the time in deep
rushing water she should lose her footing
and sink without sufficient strength to swim.
She thanked him blushing at his generous gift,
 grateful for the assurance of this aid.
Yeoman rushed upon her in a woosh
from hovering high above the Terebinth
and said that he could spot a cloud of dust
approaching from the way that they had come.
Though the hunters pace had fallen off,
gaining ground now while they'd rested here.
Quickly Kóre set upon the path
toward the sound of water trickling down.

Down, down they wound. The vegetation
thickening all the while of descent,
as did the air, suffocating under
moisture's thick blanket hoisted atop
the valley's twisting spine. The ground grew spongier,
and each successive step grew more labored
for Kóre in her now ruined moccasins
pulling free from suctioning marshy mud,
each lift an escape, each step a sucking trap.
And true to Absalom's word it wasn't long
before she tired, and weariness turned to loathing.
Sweat-drawn insects in incessant hover

around her head at least became a past-time
for Yeoman, riding along on Kóre's shoulder,
little snacks and target practice too,
helping pass the crawling minutes sloshing
onward. Plateau thoughts passed through her mind,
but only fleetingly for well she knew
to turn back would require a traverse
through torturous pathways now behind them,
and too, without a doubt she would find
Jezebel waiting at the mouth
of the valley trail with her hounds.
A bitter thing began to happen then.
Sharp stinging bites from something slithering
in the dank water began to plague
her legs. Swiping away the unseen critters,
they seemed to her small swimming serpents,
barely larger than worms, but delivering
a frightful sensation of sharp swelling pain
like stinging nettles. Panic began to well
up inside her, a pressure demanding release.
By instinct or memory or plain dumb luck
Kóre began to sing loudly at the top
of her lungs simple songs of praise to the God
of Mount Horeb, of the great Juniper
and Terebinth, and as she did, the biting
suddenly ceased and the slimy creatures scattered.
Emboldened by this discovery, Kóre sang
on and on for over an hour, inviting
Yeoman to join in, which he did

in his owlish hooting kind of way.
After they had both fallen silent,
wearied from singing on top of the trudge,
there was no sign of the pestering serpents.
But in time as silence gave way to more
vivid awareness which invited pity
which turned slowly as it does to ripe
resentment into anger into sullen
despair, like flies to manure, like road kill
calling down the vultures, the bitter
emotions called out invitation to
the murky-water serpents to return
and resume their torturous swarm
around Kóre's unprotected legs!
To which she responded once again
in furious songs of praise and, once again,
as her spirit lightened and her mind
turned toward the big God brooding over
her even though she could not see Him there,
the slithering serpents scattered. Drawn they were
to despair but repelled by praise and thanks.
Kóre realized it wasn't so much the singing
but the mind that made the difference. Self-
pity is a thinking choice, an act
of will, a deliberate opening of the curse.
Praise, which has the peculiar benefit
of taking attention off of oneself awhile,
carried the antidote that would fend
off the foul unseen slitherers of the marsh.

This realization gave to Kóre
fresh empowerment for the tiring task
at hand. She resolved to keep a steady
hand and eyes that would keep looking up
while trudging through smudge and toil and drag,
and bear it quietly. Feel it. Wear it now.
And know all trails have their starts and ends
as do trials, toils. Starts and ends.
When a thing begins another ends.
And she could persevere the lowland stench
and for the passage be the marshland wench.

Meanwhile back at the Tangling Terebinth
Jezebel and her noisy entourage
arrived. The hounds surrounded the wide tree
with frantic sniffing and confirming low growls.
She was here and not so long ago
Jezebel muttered to no one in
particular, *and she has descended*
into the stinking Bogland, has she?
Absalom was watching silently
above her, well hidden in the thick leaves.
No one can last long in such misery!
We shall split up. I will take the road
across the High and Mighty Plateau. I know
it well and shall arrive on the far side
of the marsh before Kóre can cross,

if even she can make it that far. You
(pointing to two of the grizzled dog-handlers)
wait here should Kóre give up the muck
and come seek higher dryer ground again.
She snapped her whipped with a screech and off
she bolted toward the Pride Plateau, the dogs
and soldiers following desperately behind.

Into night Kóre slogged and glad
for the coolness of the evening. But they pressed
ahead without the luxury of rest
for there was no place to lie down and dry.
This would be a night for marching on
and sleep-walking if for a minute or two
they were lucky enough to drift into
another state of mind. The morning light
revealed the awful sight: monotony
of more of yesterday without an end
in sight. The thought of one more day knee-deep
in churlish mud and thick reed swamp was sheer
despair. But quickly Kóre forced her mind
away and up with a zesty song recounting
mighty acts of God in creating the world.
Yes, He had even created bogs!
And therewith Kóre insured for awhile
a vile-slithering-serpent-free morning.
Yeoman decided on a different tact

in order to bring hope to the long-suffering
wayfarer in the muck. *I have a plan,*
he began, wing tip combing through
one of his pointy eyebrow tufts.
Now might I return your kindest favor
for all this way allowing me to ride
nestled dry here upon your shoulder.
Here is my idea that should work:
let us weave these hardy reeds together,
everywhere around us in this swamp,
tight and many, crisscrossed bit by bit.
In so doing we form a littler saucer
upon which floating net then you can sit,
and I, with leading strings of three-strand grass
as a handy rope with which to tow,
can fly and pull you skimming on this marsh
in a manner we can easily go
all day long and at a higher speed!
I'll have to spell and rest my wings, for sure,
but that is all that I will need, and you
my thoroughly drenched trampled-of-heart tramp,
can rest until we finally reach the end.

Kóre laughed out loud and marveled again
at her determined eagle owl friend,
just as splattered as she was, and feathers
make for harder cleaning. Still he thought
of her as more important than himself,
a trait so noble, even in the swelter

of the swamp. Yeoman looked to her
the king of birds. And with a refreshed hope
(for seeing what seems hopeless with new eyes
has amazing medicinal qualities!)
they worked magic with the reeds and grass
to make a marshland sleigh. Yeoman took
the grass reign in his beak and rose upon
the humid air with Kóre in tow behind.
And so they passed the second day in the Bog
which turned now more adventure than of pain
and by the fall of evening they arrived
at the far end of the wet valley's length
and to firm ground again with grass and rock,
familiar earth, putting things aright.
And just beyond— a meadow with a pond
cradling water clear, its surface a mirror,
into which the splattered duo stared
and saw themselves survivors of the Bog!
Covered head to foot with speckled mud,
they were hardly recognizable
as themselves. Yeoman looked a lot
like a flying stump of wood, and Kóre
something out of a childhood fairy tale,
and she playing the part of the fearsome troll
stumbling out of woods into the light.
Such a sight was startling and the two
starting bellying laughing at the strangeness
of it all, but strange in a way that made
them feel more at home than ever

with each other. How the cool clean water
made for the travelers such a welcome gift
to bathe their bodies, wash their clothes, and find
a fresh release on life for Horeb's flight.
Kóre hung her clean wet clothes upon
the generous branches of a Sycamore
standing stately at the meadow's end
where the path divided, like before,
to the left and right, requiring
their discernment which would need wait
until morning. A bite of angel cake,
a drink of the last water from the jar,
and to a night of sleep huddled in
a nest of leaves that Yeoman ruffled up
to cover shivering Kóre from the night.

FOUR:

ZACCHAEUS,
KEEPER OF THE SYCAMORE AT KAIROS JUNCTION

———————

The morning showed the Sycamore spreading out
a wide and glorious canopy of green
above a massive trunk twelve feet
wide, flaked in layered crusty bark-skin
holding firm a handsome skeleton
of branches lithe and confident on which
the leaves, unconcerned, hung to live
their short lives playing frivolously in the breeze.
From high and out of view a loud shout broke:
Pilgrims on the pathway fleeing trouble
I presume? Hustle up the ladder
I am lowering and come tell the matter
to me up here in my room. On the double!
A kindly bearded face from high in the tree
hurriedly motioned them upwards on the rope-
ladder dangling on one side. And now
becoming more accustomed to encounters
with the Keepers of the Trees, young Kóre
trusting this again would be for good,
climbed, though it was harder than it looked,
Yeoman in the air behind her back
helping with a little push now and then.
And so they came at last to a little house
built up high in a camouflaged ring of leaves,
simple quarters, comfortable enough.
Zacchaeus offered tea and introduced
himself as the Keeper of the Sycamore at
Kairos Junction, just south of the shore

of the wide and miserable Bogland marshes.
He was peculiarly short and stout but beamed
like one whose soul had of a past been freed.
Sipping tea, and nibbling angel cakes,
with blackberries from the tree-house cupboards,
Kóre told Zacchaeus her long tale
and asked the way to Horeb from his tree.
Pointing to the left, then, he began:

The easy Road of Greed looks at first
as the way preferable to take.
Lush it is and promises to make
an easy-going, low-fruits ripe to burst,
and shade unbroken. Heed, it is the worst
way you could choose for Horeb's sake
and for your own. Make no mistake:
the greedy vines that hang from trees long-cursed
along the very lane you would be keeping
will in the dead of night, while you lie sleeping,
wrap you in their clutches like a snake
coils the mouse before swallowing it whole.
And though you thrash to break free from the hold
the grip will tighten with every move you make.

The vines that hang are drawn by your desires,
though good at first, grow sick when they become
an end themselves and not the means toward some-
thing worthy of a human. Then as fires
feast on dry dense grass hills (till they tire

only after all the fuel is done)
the vines entwine with a lust that overcomes
resistance, weakening it as they grow tighter,
never running out of food, for there
is always more to want and more to have.
The having bores. The getting is the drug
that gives the thrill but rises like hot air
and disappears soon after the initial grab.
The beautiful once owned tilts toward ugly.

The having bores a hole right through your skull
and out will drop your heart and roll away,
disintegrating at high rate of decay,
replaced by wide eclectic collectibles.
The first range of feelings will feel full,
but they so slightly will begin to fade
until a gnawing emptiness remains,
expanding, leaving no space. It is a cruel
way to die. I know. I almost did,
helpless in the vines that I'd collected
until He invited me out and up to lunch.
The vines let go upon the words He said,
and this my one chance left, so was my hunch,
I followed Him, an act I've not regretted.

Even now you stare at the lane of trees.
Draws you, doesn't it, with a beckoning sweet?
So was the Sirens' song Odysseus beat
with wax in the ears of those who could cut him free.

I will give you a counter melody:
a song of the camel who refused retreat
at the Needle's bid to enter and eat.
He shed his bags and shaved his hump to see
if it was enough to pass. He needed more:
by an ancient spell handed down through time
he turned himself, like Midas, into gold.
The people rushed and pieces of him tore
and took him through the gate with miserly hold!
In this manner the camel passed through the Eye.

Zacchaeus stopped to gauge his listeners' interest
and found their rapt attention to each word
taut like the lifeline that in fact it was.
About to start his next extolling of
the mountain trail to the right (by pilgrims
called Stooping on the Steeps, by scoffers called
the Path of the Stupid), the way he would point
that best led towards Horeb's sheltered Cave,
he stopped suddenly at the sound below
of rushing leaves and breaking twigs: a roar
of a careless hell-bent crowd crushing through
the forest at an arrogant speed: barking
hounds at the lead of the dour company,
grim soldiers, spears as walking sticks,
and a disheveled Queen in a chariot of gold,
mirroring the look of its Queen in dirt and scrape,
the wild woman, ranting as might at night
underneath a full moon's lulling spell

the graveyard lunatic, darting eyes,
cursing *Kóre, Kóre, damnable waif!*
The hounds gathered at the Sycamore
and worked themselves into a foaming fury.
Jezebel, her hand raised, stopped the train
and peered up into the Sycamore's heart.
Kóre's heart was pounding, Yeoman froze
as still as a hallway marble statuette.
Zacchaeus nibbled on his sweet blackberries
completely unperturbed by the sudden
intrusion of the dreaded enemy into
their sweet and peaceful morning conversation.
He leaned over, whispering with a smile,
Not to worry. None can see us here,
for the ring of leaves that cover us
are hallowed and cast shadows back upon
any shadow-casting presence near.
<u>And</u> I pulled the ladder after you!
There is nothing Jezebel can do!

The hounds kept barking and scratching at the tree,
but Jezebel, convinced that she could see
through it to the top, assumed the dogs
had marked the latest encampment of her prey.
To the left she looked and saw the lane
with luscious vines, with track luxuriantly laid,
and drawn to it herself, she was convinced
Kóre too would have hurried down this way.
She pointed with her crooked finger: *On!*

And so the handlers pulled the dogs away
from the Sycamore that drew them still,
and now onto the Road of Hungry Vines
(for so it was also often called).
The beastly party trampled ahead beside
the hanging vines that seemed to slightly sway
as they passed, perhaps because they moved
the air with their rumbling mass, or then
again, it might have been the vines early
coiling at the scent of entering meat.
The grunts and yells and yelps began to fade
until the quiet calmed the tremoring air.
Zacchaeus, fumbling in the cupboard for
a toothpick, turned around and with a grin
told his friends he still had more to say:

The Mountain Trail of Mercy is the right
route to Horeb, passing through in constant rise
the precarious cliffs called the Eye for Eyes
that many have fallen from the horrible height.
O you must be careful in your flight
to stay centered on the path, for high it flies
into wild wind and constant rock slides.
Footing is treacherous, edge barriers slight.
The climb will tire you out for mercy costs.
See, payment must be made for every debt;
mercy grants the other's debt be yours
and what to them is gain becomes your loss,
and what you carry they may soon forget

in their freedom, while your pain endures.

Mercy makes the mathematician mad
for here the equation stands not on its own
but finds its answer by a gracious loan
that need not be repaid which is to add
an undeservedness some say is bad:
enabling the falling of the falling one,
rewarding the failure, feeding the moan,
leading sorrow off toward more, more sad.
Mercy disagrees and triumphs over
law and justice without undercutting
their legitimate demands in the reckless favor
of life begetting life by dying, flooding
the plains of failure with the hope there'll be
more harvest at the end than eye can see.

The greater must perfect the lesser. So
soul must call the body higher up.
Only God can teach us all to love.
Mercy tutors Justice and will go
beyond its claims to fulfill its goal:
that in the end we will all speak of
how all is well and it will be enough,
else we are back to grasping, and we know
the end of grabbing is to face the law
that power wins and money equals power,
and the ensuing fight to reach the top
as first will breed a war that will not stop

until there is no autumn harvest at all:
barren plain, no wheat, no grain, no flour.

At its zenith the path will open east:
a pasture where the sheep are lying down
beside quiet streams and all around
a table will be set for you to feast,
a sumptuous fare meticulously pieced,
replenishing your strength that will have wound
low from the long climb. The warm sound
of laughter and dishes' clink will increase
in strength across the air in radiant rings
to where in vines on the lower road will lie
your glutted enemy and she will hear
the unfettered joy that mercy brings.
You'll look to the far edge of the sky
and see Horeb's pinnacle shimmering there.

Unlike the dread that fell at the last tree
when Absalom described the Bog ahead,
Kóre's spirits soared to see the feast
in the imagination of her eye.
Invited then to spend the night aloft
in the cloaked and ringed-round high-set haven,
Kóre settled in to watch the dusk
wash the sky in glowing gradients spread
to welcome soon the fast approaching moon.

Yeoman found a perch high in the tree
from which he could scout the wide terrain
surrounding east and west the Sycamore.
Far away his keen eyes on the prowl
spotted curling of a thread of smoke
lazily lifting upward toward the stars
escaping from the net of hungry vines
spread throughout the forest like a web
in which Jezebel, as night time fell,
must be seeking fire to bring her aid.
Around the other way Yeoman spied
the steep and meandering path of Mercy's climb
into daunting mountains framed by cliffs
of exquisite height and which would be
the frame through which their travels soon would take.

Bittersweet was the ritual of goodbye
to now beloved Zacchaeus and his home
high up in the sheltered Sycamore
after breakfast and gathering things together.
Horeb called and Jezebel no doubt
would soon retrace her steps on her mistake
being understood, if she survived
the Hungry Vines at all. So to the trail
they took! The water jar again was full,
and fresh fruit accompanying the cakes
made the future bright. With fond farewells

Kóre following Yeoman set upon
the long ascent of the Mercy Trail step by step.

As it is with climbing, pace was slow,
but progress was marked by turning around
and seeing larger landscapes with each turn
laying out beneath them, stretching toward
the hazy edges of the sprawling world.
Up again with eyes trained on the trail,
taking care to keep in the middle way,
avoiding edges where the mountain fell
down into deep chasms beyond seeing.
Once Kóre dared peer over the edge
and shouted out *hello*! into the abyss.
The echo that returned was dark and cold,
a scoffing hurl that mocked her little frame,
hell for you! is how the voice returned.
The bottom of the drop could not be seen,
but the chill of the judgement cliffs bit clean.
With a shudder Kóre turned away
and resolved to not look down anymore.
At end of day what was a breeze picked up
heft and swirled the path dust in a dance.
In raucous gusts with lulls between it blew
as if to throw the balance of Kóre afoul
and feed her toward a leering precipice.
Soon the gusts gave way to steady push
and a garbling buffeting of the ears
where Kóre couldn't hear her own voice yell.

Yeoman had long given up his flight
and clung with mighty talons to the straps
of the pack Kóre carried on her back.
Into night the duo labored on
against the sparring wind and growing chill
until they found shelter where they could rest
underneath an A-frame of two boulders—
a providential tent up to the task
of standing against the constant bullying wind.
Here they slept and wondered if the wind
would quiet in the morning, which it did,
yielding to another day of climbing,
yet at an incline steeper than before.
Mercy Trail grew the more demanding
the longer one was on it, so it seemed.
Aching legs and blistering feet the price
of pressing steadily on toward afternoon
when once again the winds returned to taunt
their tired bodies and their faltering steps.
But undaunted, carried by the vision
of the feast that would await their ascent
to the top, they trudged on toward the meadow
Zacchaeus said was there. By later day
the winds were at their peak and pieces of
slate were sloughing off the mountain walls
and crashing down around them on the path.
The howl of wind made hearing impossible,
and eyes were squinted tight against the lash,
making falling-rock detection guesswork.

Pieces of slate like a critic's searing words
plagued the air and crashed all around
the duo bent into the beguiling wind.
Upon a rock recently fallen in
the middle of the trail, Kóre tripped
and fell heavily to the ground with Yeoman
still clinging to her back. They lay there
for several minutes in the exhaustion of fight.
A stinging burn drew Kóre to touch her knee,
her hand returned with smear of blood. The fall
had dealt a gash, how deep could not be told.
As she reached to wrap it with a cloth,
a mountain boulder as large as a small house
thundered down from above and with a shock-
wave of dust and shard landed squarely
in the middle of the path right where they would
have been had not Kóre fortuitously tripped!
Pulverized in a flash would have been their fate
had not providence another end
in mind, using even the instrument
of wound to avoid the merciless hammer of death.
Stunned by the blast, and even more
by the realization of the grace
surrounding them, Kóre cried out loudly,
Save us, King of Horeb! As you have
and will again! Mercy on us now
and onward through the falling rock and wind!
With rush of adrenaline and dogged eyes
full of determination, Kóre rose

and scrambled up the fallen boulder lying
right in front of them, still oozing dust.
On the top of the boulder the wind was fierce,
but there were finger holds along the crevices
of the face of the fallen giant
to which Kóre clung with iron grip,
scampering over and to the other side.
The shaken pilgrims leaned into the wind,
shaking off the fear of flying slate,
and step by step ascended the treacherous way.
Finally by nightfall, they approached
what proved to be the final bend and found
the promised meadow nestled in a ring
of perched high rocks, protected from the wind,
like a nest, and there the tables sat,
flush with meats and cheeses, beer and wine,
such a spread of fruits in bowls of crystal:
peaches, grapes, and huckleberries,
apple of varied stripe, banana, mango,
sweet coconut, plums and apricots.
Almonds, walnuts, and pistachio
in piles next to still warm honey bread,
sauces for dipping and pouring, green
salads of cucumber and ripest tomato—
a banquet set for an army of hungry men!
The spotless white cloths draping the tables
were lined in lace weave of intricate design.
The candelabras, lit with dancing flames,
were gold and of a workmanship unlike

anything that Kóre had ever seen before,
a symmetry of swirl over detailed etchings
telling stories of war and victory.
The strangest feature of the idyllic scene
was the ringing silence. After wind's
unrelenting roar, the silence seemed
loud. Odd it was that no one there
hosted over the tables finely set.
All was perfect. All was quiet. All
was what Kóre imagined heaven to be.

FIVE:

DEBORAH,
KEEPER OF THE PALM OF
PLENTY

In the middle of the refuge field
stood a lone tree like Saruman's tower,
strange and out of place: a Palm it was,
with a thick trunk wide around and ribbed,
fat at bottom, thinning toward the top
where burst in fans the great and spiked leaves,
above the collar of past seasons' slain
hanging on, brown and brittle, solemn
memorial to yesterday's life. The coconuts,
tucked in bunches underneath the span
of the windmill wings in wind alive,
their coarse hides knocked in the evening breeze
a steady rhythm at the heart of the scene.
Strung from the top of the tree there hung a swing
in which sat a beautiful warrior Queen,
gently swaying back and forth and back,
a coat of armor covering her breast,
a helmet made of gold, inlaid with stones—
starry jasper, gold tiger's eye,
snowflake obsidian to name a few—
which framed her chiseled cheeks in austere light,
and she looked as handsome as a god,
watching as the strangers entered in
the meadow of the feast laid. With a grin
she cried words of welcome, bid them come
closer to the Palm Tree that she might
find out what business brought them to
the Meadow Fair and Plenty at the end

of the Mercy Trail. And thus she cried:
Do not linger at the outskirts there
for from here I cannot see your faces.
Owl and lady, draw now near to me
so I can tell you all of what this place is,
and you can tell to me your journey tale,
why you've come and climbed the arduous hill.

Kóre cautiously approached the Palm,
hoping that this Keeper would be like
the others that had helped her on her way.
On the telling of her Horeb-bound trek
and the reason for it, Deborah smiled
and offered her wise counsel and more beside,
introducing herself as the Keeper
of the Palm of Plenty. She would now
direct the pair the best way to descend
the mountain safely, a route that then would lead
expediently onward toward Horeb's plain.
Her first words were warning, clear and strong,
that another path would at the first seem right:

The steep and most direct descent begins
there beside the pile of greying boulders
and drops precipitously at that shoulder;
the earth is loose and slippery at the bend.
Envy Slide (the most joyless of all sins)
is its name and has been since days older
when first brother's love by it grew colder.

70

The elder killed the younger over a sense
of being bested. So he fought and lost
his destiny though he won his fight.
Here is not to aspire but surpass
and exceed the other at all cost.
The other's joy becomes an odious sight,
driven by need to be the first and last.

This descending slope is shrouded thick
with a fog the sun cannot burn free,
locking in the visibility
to just beyond the span of a walking stick.
The blinding lack of sense gives rise to quick
judgments of survival for the "me."
Whatever good to be found, it must be
kept for self in case of trial or trick.
The mist divides companions first by eye,
and if not by sight, by darkened heart.
The pale begins to hypnotize the mind
that what is good will be in short supply
and all must be grabbed up right from the start.
It is but self-betrayal to be kind.

Along that wash there will be no stream.
Water is the sign of gratitude
(the way it flows in joyful plentitude)
and envy will not spare the breath to deem
a gain as gift. Otherwise would seem
inappropriate and blatantly rude

to withhold thanks from whom thanks is due.
Envy rages on, just like her Queen
Jezebel, that grace is for the weak
and gratefulness is spreading armor wide
to allow the enemy free his thrust.
To give thanks is to admit defeat,
admitting to the need of one beside,
admitting life is better lived by trust.

There have been more murders on this trail
than on any other. Here is why:
envy leads to hatred faster by
its working poison than anger or greed will.
To despise the sight of another's well-
being is the core of hatred. High
the price that hate will not deny.
And high the price the heart will pay which fails
to forbid when envy's squatting first
appears. For once it settles in, eviction
is a most unpleasant messy task.
Skeletons will line the path and worse:
the stench of hate in fog-induced constriction
will suffocate all fools who try to pass.

Kóre stared out toward the greying boulders
and could spot the very falling away
of which Deborah warned in such grave terms.
Surely there must be another way
to descend this mountain and stay safe?

To this Deborah laughed and cried, *Of course!*
But first she insisted on a break.
After such a most distasteful speech
she was in the mood for coconut
and wondered if her guests would like the treat.
She began to share how rare were these
fruits grown from the seeds handed down
from the trees in Eden (no, she said,
these were not THE fruit, and then she winked!).
These were coconuts whose flesh was sweet
and hearkened back to the days of innocence.
Eating them would fill the spirit up
with hunger for an exquisite holiness,
an eagerness to stay pure on the road.
But as well would place deep in the soul
an agonizing sorrow that would bid
a fountain fall of tears for what could not
be fully expressed. Sorrow for the lost
goodness of a world now buried in rot,
sorrow for the sorrow of the One
Who had first on the canvas of the Not
called it all to Be with beautiful strokes
what it was His mind delighted to see.
Kóre took a bite and felt the rush
of sweetness, strong and ruddy, welling up,
followed by an avalanche of tears
that she was unembarrassed to let out.
Yeoman, wondering if the effect would take
on an owl too, bit and found the same

rush of tangled emotion for he too
was the handiwork of Him who cried.
Awash in tears, and now with Deborah too,
weeping unashamed while covered by
a holy sweetness, Deborah now began
to point a way toward Horeb other than
the dark disintegrating Slide of Envy.

The safe descent begins on a trail of tears:
see it on the opposite side of the field?
Tears are sacraments of in revealed—
signs of either joy or sorrow. Here
the catalyst for weeping is most clear:
on the Empathy Path you will feel
what another feels in a way so real
that it sparks the genuine tear appear.
To step into another's shoes as if
they were one's own is an imagination
sanctified. It sets apart the mind
from the narrow boundaries, cramped and stiff,
of the self alone: an invitation
to enter another's world, to feel and find.

To say "that could be me" is to enlist
the company of gratitude and grace.
Another's trouble sits in another place
now, tomorrow it could become my test.
The tears of Empathy, though, are not just
selfish fear of what I might need face.

Rather a sharing now of another's aches
imperfectly but real, it will insist.
One can bear the sorrow of a friend
by entering underneath the pain without
solutions, easy answers. Quiet presence,
deep concern, permission to allow
the suffering to be felt to the end.
Waiting alongside is this essence.

Same it is with joy. Real empathy
feels the thrill of the other's true success
and celebrates it, does not wish it less
than all it could be. Feels no jealousy
and wastes no time comparing history.
It wishes for the other all the best
and even stands to guard against what presses
to eclipse the other's full joy spree.
Its own voice will add congratulation.
Its own song will sing the other's praise.
In the night the sweetness of the pleasure
of the other's joy brings relaxation
and the sleep of peace into the coming day
without hint of envy's spoiling pressure.

You will find the trail with benches hewn,
on which you can sit and see the way
winding on below you where will play
the journey of the ones ahead of you,
a chance for you to rest as others move,

increasing the gap between you and they.
Use the bench to practice celebrating
the good progress of the others. As you do,
the trail's descent will grow the sweeter still,
and you will begin to see in the trees beside,
the coconuts of which you just have eaten
easily accessed, as much as you will,
food for strength and to soften the ride,
tears of joy and sorrow to smooth, to sweeten.

Kóre felt such peace here in this Meadow
of Fair and Plenty at the bountiful tables
full of luscious treats and pleasant air.
Too the company of Deborah was
such that gave Kóre courage in her gut.
How she wished that Jezebel would turn
up in this Meadow and have to face
this warrior sitting poised upon the swing.
Now having laid out the full scheme
of what lay ahead, Deborah exclaimed:
O but what a terrible host I've been—
filling you with long discourse before
inviting you to feast and drink your fill!
To the tables, friends, and let us toast
the glad success of your journey to this point
and drink to its fulfillment one day soon
upon arriving at the Cave of Horeb!
Deborah's snapping back to the present time
stirred Kóre's suppressed hunger back

into full awareness, anticipation.
The threesome gathered around the tables and ate
and laughed and drank and ate and ate even more.
Kóre noticed that the more she ate
her hunger dissipated but she never
felt the sickening sensation of growing full.
She and Yeoman could enjoy the wide
spread of taste and texture for as long
as they desired, such was the magic
of this wonderful Meadow on the mountain.
Soon the hour grew late and night had fallen,
and Deborah bid farewell, time to return
to the upper Palms to spend the night.
She would invite the travelers up to sleep
except there was no room there, save for her.
But she gave them leave to sleep beneath
the cover of the banqueting tables. There
she said the sleep would be most peaceful
and at the mourning dove's first greeting coo
to hurry to the Path of Empathy
for the way the light fell in the dawn
would give them clearest clues how to begin.
And then to follow the benches, and rest often,
she assured them they would make the plain
before the fall of night, such was the track.
The warm embracing of the Warrior Queen
once more called forth tears from both and then
off to sleep, underneath the tables,
renewing their strength and readying for the march

down the mountain and toward Horeb's gate.

The morning was awash in the song of birds.
A flock of robins washing in the stream
hailed the day as come and full of good.
The sunlight fell directly into Kóre's
eyes, and why? Strangest thing of all:
the banqueting tables last night set so full
were nowhere to be seen! Not even prints
in the meadow grass to prove that they
had been standing laden with food the night
before. Yeoman flew around the Meadow;
the tables all had vanished in the night.
Probably a good thing, Kóre thought,
or else I might be sore tempted to linger
past the time of the mourning dove's calling card,
which could make discovering Empathy harder,
or even lead to mistaking it for Envy's Slide
and find myself in peril on that side.
Kóre rose and looked up to the tree
but Deborah and her swing were out of sight.
Heartsick at the thought of moving on,
nevertheless across the field they set,
past the boulders leading Envy's way.
Kóre shuddered at the thought of the fog
that lay below the brink of that foul ridge.
The light filtering through the high Palm's crown

latticed on the ground a pattern toward
a clump of bushes on the meadows edge,
on the rim and overlooking the world.
Yeoman, up ahead, confirmed that this
was indeed the Path of Empathy
that would lead them safely to the plain,
for an old bench sat below the brow
of the hill insuring this the way.
Down they went. At first the trail was steep,
with passages of stair-stepped rocks to drop
along the precarious curves and edges sharp
of the sheer wall sides of the mountain pass.
Soon they came upon an old stone bench,
lichen lined, with carvings of a lion
on the four stone legs on which it sat.
Following Deborah's word they paused to sit
awhile to rest and see what they could see.
Across the valley there the path could be
faintly sketched out on the yonder face,
and figures moving up and down upon
it, going about their own peculiar way
with the steadiness of purpose, so
it seemed. The motion moved like in a dance
to Kóre watching, intricate and sweet,
as if in every next frame purposes
neared completion in a cosmic scheme
underneath a musical waving hand
fingering a baton. On they hiked,
down the steep and stair-pocked winding trail

to join the hillside's movement, up and down.
The pitch soon eased somewhat, the way widened
and trees with coconuts on branches low
growing out of the hill along the path
offered real refreshment, joy and tears.
And every time it seemed that weariness
grew conspicuous, a bench did too,
for more rest, more watching down the way
life in movement, but of what could not
be told, for always that the yonder scene
was far enough to blur particulars,
and whether they were deer or mountain goats,
or sheep, or horse, or mule, or even men,
Kóre could not tell, but that they were,
and that they mattered in the wider scheme.
The stranger part was, though they descended fast,
expecting each next turn to meet the folk
whom they had seen above, it never was
the case. At each round the trail was quiet,
empty of the travelers spotted above,
though the marks of scuff were everywhere,
and the scent of flesh, though faint, remained.
But never an encounter! Yeoman thought
to fly across the valley from one bench
and hurry upon the distant scene to see
the moving characters up close, but Kóre
thought this act would be a forcing of
a narrow perspective on a wider scene
that could warp a delicate balance in play.

Nay, she said, *but let us take what comes*
as it comes and with that be content,
whether or not it comes as we expect.
For we too on our own part are intent,
and to be faithful thus is to respect
that doing our part is the best that can be done.
And so they went in turns on foot, at rest,
slowly down the way all by themselves,
when suddenly behind them footsteps scratched
the evening still with a quick determined pace.
Stopping to look behind, Kóre waited
nervously to see who would round the bend.
A small figure (whether boy or girl
Kóre could not tell) came into view,
face cloaked in a hood, and looking down.
On the shoulder of the traveler sat
a squawking blue jay goading on the child
with an irritating *Keep on Erok,*
keep on, Erok, keep on Erok, keep on!
Hurriedly they past Yeoman and Kóre
without looking up or giving a word
of greeting. Kóre attempted a *hello*
which was brusquely ignored as on they walked
at fast pace, this odd pair of pilgrims.
Kóre felt an anger rising up
within her. Why would they act this way?
Did she think herself better than they?
And now they were ahead of them on the path
and would make it down before they would.

And what if they were also on the way
to Horeb and would take up the last space
in the Cave? Kóre felt the urge
to run ahead and overtake the hooded
figure and her bird with perhaps
a snide comment to put them in their place,
when at that moment they came upon a bench.
The last thing Kóre wanted to do was sit
again and wait and watch her undeserving
fellow traveler take up space ahead.
As she moved to pass on by the bench,
Yeoman shouted: *Stop, Kóre, and look up!*
The urgency in his owl voice clipped
her movement short, and looking up she saw
wisping overhead a murky fog
channeling down through a cleft in the mountainside
and swirling right above them. *Envy Slide*
must pass very close to Empathy Path
near here and its poisonous air can reach
this far. Let us spend some minutes on
the bench and eat the flesh of Coconut
for we are in need of a counteracting measure!
Kóre saw immediately Yeoman's point
and hurried to the bench, her soul amiss
with a growing hatred for the stranger
and the bird that had so indecorously
passed them by. Upon the bench a calm
descended on them both. They looked to see
down the path and what would soon become

of their odd counterparts. Looking
around the far bend, far ahead, where
they should next appear, nothing at all!
They waited curious with now-still hearts.
Nothing. Nowhere on the path below
were the strangers to be seen at all.
Now chewing on the coconut, with tears
of sadness replacing the earlier snarl, Kóre
wondered if the entire episode
had been in fact a phantom projected by
the profane fog of Envy overhead.
Perhaps the couple had been a mental mirror
of Kóre and Yeoman themselves, the dark poison
turning them against themselves by turning
them against the idea of someone else.
Shaking her head, Kóre rose up from
the bench of rescue and continued on her way,
Yeoman flapping away any remnant wisps
of the fog of Envy loitering near.
Steady on from there on even pace,
the way increased in ease with every step
and by the time the sun was half-cupped on
the world's rim with orange spread and red,
with Kóre's shadow longer than her twice,
the trail flattened out and narrowed down
into a canyon with a dry rock bed
as its floor, and for a mile it led
outward toward the wide desert plain
stretching on in rippled shadows toward

Horeb's distant rise. At the canyon's
mouth the way was blocked from side to side
by a towering Tamarisk whose branches
filled the entire space between the walls
from low near the ground to canyon top,
making like a gate. Flying above
Yeoman scouted two trails on the other
side setting into desert space:
one veered left, the other, better kept,
veered off to the right in straight route.
As it now was night, as times before,
waiting until morning made much sense.
Jezebel seemed like a far-off dream,
and a hope arose in Kóre's breast
that maybe this tree too was kept by one
who could help them know which way to go.

SIX

SAUL,
KEEPER OF THE SKELETON
TAMARISK

In the middle of the night a sound
like the rattling of loose sticks in a bag
woke Kóre from her dreaming sleep,
and what she saw appeared as if a dream
still. A window in the Tamarisk trunk
had opened inward and there in the hole
was a smiling skull (or so it seemed
a smile, with its wide angular jawbone
holding out a yellow- toothy grin)
crowned with long grey hair pulled in a tail
and wrapped round with a band of scarlet silk.
Child and owl-friend, do not be alarmed
at my frightful form, for I am bones
and yet still I live as a friend to guide
travelers who come upon this mouth
at the edge of the Desert of Dry Bones.
Saul, Keeper of the Skeleton
 Tamarisk at your service, now until dawn,
for I can only move about at night.
Daylight binds me to my tree-trunk tomb,
but every evening is rebirth again
to this world for awhile. I seek,
out of my remorse, to shed some light
on the Raging Wrath-Road and the Meek-Pale Trail,
both of which stretch out before you now
and will take you vastly different routes,
one of bubbling tar pits stinking fierce,
the other made by primordial magic stone.

Though still stunned by a speaking skeleton,
Kóre sensed the kindness in his tone,
and trusted then to tell him of her tale.
Upon hearing of her misadventure,
Saul the Skeleton urged Kóre to heed
his words and leave before the break of dawn,
for familiar as he was with death,
he could actually smell death's puppet near,
closing in by the moment he could tell.

Listen then, and listen quick and well.
To the right the well kept trail makes
a good appearance , as if best to take it,
such we think of efficiency's luring spell.
But beware, it shortcuts straight to hell:
a field of tar pits, boiling mad with hate,
each one formed by a murder, seeds which late
turn to stinking tar as bones to oil.
The Raging Road is fast but carries long
the consequence of all done in its way.
Anger fuels. It foils the pause to pray
before the sword is swung at instinct's push
and is not satisfied until the crush
of the opponent is complete and strong,

wronged enough to justify the thrust.
O there is a good anger to be sure,
a fierceness born of firmness, hot and pure,
fueled by reasons in God's eyes seen just.

Even He, with whip, raised temple dust
in overturning cages, coins that were
making mockery of the place of prayer.
But this road has nothing of this, trust
me, little one. Anger is unwieldy.
To bear it well, rare are those who can,
and no one past the setting of the sun.
As transient as is mist that rises from
the fields as morning dew to sunlight yields, see
nothing good remains in the fisted hand.

On the surface, a righteous drama shows,
but underneath is where the poison lies.
Anger seeds a hatred, guides the eyes
to spy out opportunity in which to sow
blunt misfortune, wishing one to know
agony, and why this? Why the size
of someone's sorrow should soothe another's pride?
It makes little sense, but wrath is no
respecter of fair Reason, rather feeds
off the fumes of passion, and so it is
how often eros turns to seething rage
in the space of the narrowest line, and needs
hardly an excuse toward such as this,
senseless provocation to engage.

The banks of the tar pits, marble-like, are slick,
and all those who dare near will slip in,
thinking they can manage how and when

to approach the sight. It is a trick.
Anger sucks the loiterer with a lick
and a swallow into the boiling sin
and burns mercilessly clothes and skin,
which will only make wrath more thick,
multiply self-pity to a state
making reckless choices to seem fair,
like I, calling late on Endor's Witch,
or (how could I?) taking up my spear
in madness, trying to pin him with my pitch,
he, who I loved most, I chose to hate.

Saul the Skeleton lifted up his head
and sniffed the air (without a nose who knows
how?). Suddenly— if choreographed
the timing could not have been more perfect—
the howl of hounds materialized on the breeze,
carried along from the Raging Road of Wrath!
How could Jezebel have since escaped
the Hungry Vines of Greed and then made
it around the looming cliffs to thus approach
now from the open desert? Kóre's heart
began to pound in fear and Yeoman took
to the sky to see the distance left
between them and the Tamarisk of Saul.
Dropping from the sky in free-fall form,
Yeoman with excitement in his eyes
announced the evil company to be
less than the length of Bending Birch Meadow—

a field where Kóre and the owl had played
hours and hours in much kinder times.
Follow me now, Saul hissed through old teeth,
and disappeared inside his dark tomb trunk.
Without hesitation Yeoman flew
inside and Kóre followed, barely squeezing
herself through the trifling trunk-side hole.
Eyes adjusting soon enough they saw
a ladder rising up into the dark.
Hurry! whispered Saul from somewhere up
in the black above them. Kóre climbed
as fast as she could, Yeoman fluttering
above her head, leading blind the way.
Up they went until the ladder flattened
out into a tunnel leading straight
into the rock cliff face beside the tree.
Yes, yes, this way, Saul encouraged.
Soon they came to a cave, lit with a fire.
On the rock walls all around them hung
parchments in a beautiful script Kóre
had seen before but didn't know how to read.
When they had sat down to catch their breath,
Saul, taking notice of her stares
and growing curiosity, explained:

Upon this wall are hung the inspired poems
of the one my anger sought to kill.
He refused, such was his noble will,
to follow in a manner like my own.

In this very cave I came alone
and he was hiding in the shadows still,
with ample opportunity to fill
up sweet revenge for the evil I had shown.
He chose the path of self-control and trust,
allowing God to mete out what was due,
and he, convinced that God was strong and just,
would let Him see the unmet justice through.
Against the urging of his fellow men,
he stayed his sword to let me live again.

Through this tunnel— mind you it is snug—
you will find the famous Meek-Pale Trail.
It stretches out into the desert dale
and is made of a magic gravel dug
from deep quarries underneath the mud
where the richest mineral veins prevail—
lodes of precious Peace-Stone, greenish-pale,
and worth, if I can say, the price of love.
For with this stone the martyrs jeweled their crowns,
and by it bought another way to be,
found its commerce profitable beyond
the common currency of injury,
death, and spiteful war as payments down.
Making peace they strove, and peace their song.

Ridiculed by warriors, proud, at ease,
these stone merchants meek were wiser still,
for when the warriors after war bent ill,

92

all their spoil became the spoil to these,
inheriting for their steadfast work of peace
the piles of hard-claimed loot gained in the kill.
The merchants hired craftsmen from the hills
to take the bounty of the war and piece
it all together with the green Peace-Stone
to construct over the desert sand a new
trail, leading where swords will be remade
into implements for field, and true
community will finally arrive at home
having followed the mystical Peace-Stone way.

But know my friends this way is hard and must
be travelled barefoot. Only then the stone
will work upon the feet and make known
the way across the desert's varied crust.
Meekness is a suffering of long-trust
in the invisible power of God alone
and refuses wrath to seize and own
the quick and easy solution near that must
make common sense to the offended mind.
Long the barefoot way and long the pain,
but gradually will come the dulling of
the searing burn, until some moment finds
a switch, as when the itch is scratched, the lane
will turn to joy, as labor turns to love.

Saul by now was whispering with a joy,
and for a moment Kóre swore she saw

Saul enfleshed as he in days of old
was seen and known by family and friend:
handsome, tall, and favored to be king,
chosen among all the people by God.
Clothed in skin he smiled with twinkling eyes,
and Kóre loved him greatly, and she reached
 to hug him and in doing so felt bones
again, and pulling back, the skeleton
was all to see. But now she knew he waited
for the coming age when Horeb's top
would burst a burning spill upon the world
and change it like the jeweler melts down gold
into a precious cup for Him whose lips
will drink the virgin glory and enjoy
its untarnished beauty without end,
a cup set all around with precious stones,
green-pale stones, radiant and true.

But now there was more traveling to do.
Kóre took her shoes off in the dim
cave and stowed them in her pack and set
her foot upon the gravel green stone path
leading downward into deeper dark,
but toward a cave mouth where began the Trail.
How the first steps on the path were biting.
Soft and tender foot-flesh scraped and cut
with every step, and Kóre wincing, wondered
how this way would even be possible,
seeing they were not yet to the mouth.

Saul remained behind and called out, *Slowly.*
Stop and rest. On this path you have time.
Jezebel cannot tread upon it
and your scent the green stone covers up.
Furthermore, the light glow that it casts
hides you even in the shortest span.
She will pass you by if you stand still
even though she come within arm's swipe
as long as you remain shorn of your shoes.
And so cringing, step by step she went,
Yeoman watching, suffering more than she,
in his inability to stave
off the piercing pain again, again.
In this way they came in torturous time
to the mouth that looked out wide upon
the Desert of Dry Bones as the sun arose.

Wide and open lay the panoramic
scene of desert, far as eye could reach
under cloudless sky and washed-out blue.
The baking ground, short on shade everywhere,
shimmered even though the day was young.
The Meek Pale Trail stretched out into
the yawning desert scape without a flinch
of fear for it was way and true and life.
Upon the severe green Peace-Stone the pair
ventured out into the vulnerable light

trusting Saul spoke truly that the path
would indeed miraculously shield them
from the sight of Jezebel if she
came upon them since she was close by.
Kóre's pace was crawl, was all her feet
could bear, with many stops as well to stem
each breach and burn. Until Yeoman thought
perhaps that he could half-carry Kóre on,
if she held his talons while he winged,
she being sure to keep her feet upon
the green Peace-Stone, but with hardly weight
laid upon it, such could seriously help
with the pain. And just as he imagined
so it came to be, similar to
his pulling Kóre through the odious Bogland's
endless marshes, now which seemed a time
long, long ago, but really was
only some days back. Forward now
at better pace, Kóre skimming along
the Meek Pale Trail, almost as if skating
awkwardly on ice, wobbling under
Yeoman's steady flying through the strain.
Though Kóre was light, as owls go—
he the very largest of his breed—
Yeoman's burden was significant.
But with rest stops, deep into the long
desert scape they found themselves at point
when sun was highest in the empty sky.
Stopping for a drink from Elijah's jar

(which was full as always he had said
it would be long as it remained unmixed
from any other pool), they also fed
upon the angel cakes, reviving strength
underneath the shade of a Sissoo tree
that had grown beside the Meek Pale Trail
and offered it the exquisite gift of cool.

Leaning back to back and thinking how
the journey had not been what they had feared,
shockingly upon the hot still air
the angry curls of barking reached their ears,
rolling through the shallow desert swales,
growing louder like an ocean wave
just about to crash upon the beach.
Kóre froze and prayed the green Peace-Stone
would hide them in the daylight. Soon they saw
the cloud of rising dust approaching from
the north and heading toward the Sissoo tree,
that the only source of shade in sight
in this arid stretch of stark terrain.
Barreling down upon them in a rush,
Kóre swore they'd marked her as a target,
such was the precision of their aim.
Overwhelming was the instinct in her
to up and dash away as fast as she
could run the opposite direction from
the accelerating dervish cloud. And she might
have done so were it not for Yeoman's strength,

his wings spread over her, whispering calm:
Quiet now, and we shall be quite safe!
Evil cannot touch these stones of peace.
Kóre wriggled her toes into the stones
and for the first time felt affection for
the very pain delivered by the rocks,
for now their injury was greater life,
and all their hurt was keeping for her health.
Strange how sometimes pain itself feels good
but only when the larger scales reveal
the miseries that pain has shielded from.
Wretched dogs with blood-stained eyes and sweat
arrived straining their necks in front of her,
the Queen erect within her chariot
once pristine and golden, now abused
by mud and weather, scrape of every kind,
surrounded now by eight grim surly men
attending to her hounding, to the hounds.
Jezebel looked extraordinarily worn,
sunken face, creased with dirt and smudge.
The evil in her eyes was ever bright,
(if bright can be the word describing dark)
bent on seizing what she said was hers,
unfamiliar with the otherwise
common sense of being denied a thing.
The entire party pulled up to the tree.

Watch out! Jezebel cried to her lead,
Do not touch the poisonous green stone path!

It will burn us with a burn that creeps
and crawls across the skin and will not stop
until it reaches the eyes and makes us blind.
Our apothecaries have not found
yet an ointment to retract its curse!
Do not touch it, beast or man, or I
will put you down myself in mercy kill.
For I cannot be touched by creatures who
are infected with the crawling burn.
Now, let us rest awhile right here
beneath the shade of this lonely, pitiful tree.
Can the dogs not pick up any scent?
Has not our girl passed along this way?
Release the dogs and let them scout the range
while we rest and gather up our strength.
My sense tells me we are very near,
and perhaps tonight shall trap our prey
in these Venus hands that are hungrier still
for all this time that I have had to wait.
Oh, I swear now I shall make her pay
for the inconvenience she has wrought
on my life, and wasted me these days.
Kóre shall pay dearly to her Queen.

And now what a marvelous scene it was!
To see the evil Queen against the tree
leaning up and looking straight into
the face of Kóre looking back at her
not a body length away by space

but in another dimension walled by grace.
Kóre stared now at her nemesis
and felt a nausea rising up within.
Jezebel was wrinkled at the eyes,
not from laughter but from permanent frown.
Her skin was gray and pulled back tight as if
she was held together by a pin
and once released the sum of all of her
would unravel and blow away in the wind.
Her eyes never rested, darting back
and forth as if driven by a restless haunt
or thirst. Her spindly fingers mindlessly
fidgeted a gold medallion that hung
around her neck, imprinted on both sides,
but of what Kóre could not see.
Every once in a while Jezebel
would lift the gold piece to her lips and kiss it,
muttering something in another tongue,
paying blind obeisance to some force
that held her in leash as she held her dogs.
As she breathed her rapid shallow way,
the very air around was spoiled with dank
and rottenness no words can apt describe.
The longer Kóre stared her terror dimmed
and, slight though they were at first, small rings
of pity for her rose up from true seeing.
But still she froze and dared not twinge or twitch,
waiting for this nightmare meeting to end.
At one moment Jezebel's dark eyes

narrowed as if suddenly catching view
of something somewhere there before her face.
Kóre started at the thought the Peace-Stone
magic might even now be wearing off.
But just as soon the look of focus vanished
into far-off vacancy again.
The tongue-hanging dogs sniffed aimlessly around,
failing to pick up any scent at all,
and looking more like leathered skeletons,
none of their tails wagging on their rounds.
How long the stalemate dragged, the hiding pair
could not tell, though soon their muscles ached
and begged to stretch, but still they did not move.
Finally lack of patience brought relief
as Jezebel stood suddenly and cried,
We are wasting time! What useless dogs,
what useless crew! What am I to do
surrounded by such rank incompetence?
Up she was in a burst of furious push,
on her chariot, and pointing off due south.
She cannot be far and surely in this heat
where we find some shade we shall find her.
And off in a dust-cloud of chaotic whirl,
the evil company departed. Deep
sighs of sweet relief sounded from
both the stolid owl and her young brave charge.

Up again and eastward Horeb bound
the duo headed with much daylight left.
And then it was: the most amazing thing!
Kóre as she stepped out on the Trail
again anticipating the searing pain
of the unrelenting green Peace-Stone
felt no pain upon her feet at all!
Looking down her cuts had healed over
and the bottoms of her feet looked new
 as if during the wait they'd been replaced!
What strange twist and turn was this that now
she could walk upon the road of peace,
even skip or run, like she was made
to do so from the first? Joy overtook
her heart as once again she realized
right ways are not easy but become
easier through the suffering required
until the suffering becomes a kind
of joy that none know but who first endure
the hardest stretch. At least it keeps the way
far less travelled for the many who turn
away before the turning of the pain
to light and lightness. On and on they went
now in easy conversation, Yeoman
on her shoulder, riding restfully like
a prince upon his much beloved steed,
and every moment eastward spreading space

between them and their agitated pursuers.
The wide, wide spaces which at first seem cruel
and menacing, as if to swallow them up
now appeared inviting, making room
for them within the diverse company
of the desert home: the wildflowers
in surprising patches, kangaroo rats
hiding from the snakes and leopards, lithe
experts in the art of subtle hunting.
With ibex and gazelle in timid herds
passing at a distance midst the ghaf
and abal, peeking out behind the date palms,
the desert turned friend, though stifling hot,
but heat like strong embrace instead of fire.
And so they came to evening, to the cool,
and kept upon the Meek Pale Trail as night
fell upon the land and turned the heat
to cool and quick toward cold. What fickle air!
The full moon afforded generous light
and behind it spilled stars across space,
cheering silently the wayfarers toward home.
Eating coconut saved from the mountain,
with the return of tears returned their strength,
and they resolved to push on through the night.
The green Peace-Stone glowed slightly so
to make their headway clear and without fear,
up and down through shadowed wadis they
travelled light of heart and buoyed with hope
until early morning, while still moon

managed sky and sun had not yet shown
up to take its turn for another day,
Kóre, Yeoman found the trail end,
at the edge of a bluff between two trees,
both of them the same, on either side
of where the green Peace-Stone trail stopped.
Beyond the trees the trail disappeared
over the cliff above a creviced land,
what in the night looked like severe cracked skin
magnified enormous. As before
Kóre weighed the cost of pushing ahead
without sufficient knowledge and declared
the risk was too great to stubbornly proceed.
Looking at the two trees at this junction,
Kóre guessed there might be another Keeper
to advise them how best to advance.
She called out despite the early hour
and hoped the hospitality would be
matched as she so far had fairly found.

SEVEN

NATHANIEL & SIMON,
TWIN KEEPERS OF THE FIGS AT OVERLOOK BLUFF

———————————

Ho, there! Is a Keeper here to tell
us which of these two paths is best to go?
Kóre cried out in an eager voice.
From above, right, high up, she heard
a rustling in the leaves and gentle call:
Just a moment please! I'll be right down!
And so will I! another voice from left,
squeaky, high-pitched, quite unlike the first
which had sounded calm and confident.
Leaf-rake rustling dribbled down either side,
until appeared from both trees Keepers two
who seemed eager to be the first to greet
the weary travelers with their welcoming
though the dawn was still an hour away.
Peace there, friends, the kind and lanky one
to their right spoke first, dark-complexioned,
marked by composure. *Nathaniel is*
my name and you have come to Overlook Bluff
on the border of the Wastelands Maze.
Almost interrupting him the other
Keeper piped up, *I am Simon. This*
fig tree to your left, my home and yours!
Come and stay awhile and rest with me.
I am famed for magic tricks that take
your minds off trouble with a chip of cheer.
He was short and bald with bright red cheeks,
standing hunched which seemed to be caused by
his belly weight that pulled him toward the ground.

Simon reached toward Kóre, gesturing toward
his tree, but Yeoman flew between the two,
quite uncertain of this stranger's bent.
Nathan laughed. *Don't mind my zealous friend.*
Company for us out here is rare.
Simon has forgotten his manners much
as he did upon first seeing Her.
But that is a story for another time.
With that he gave a look of severity
to which Simon scowled and backed a pace.
Deep set eyes that had both power to calm
or rattle the soul this Nathaniel had.
Simon speaks a truth, but I say more.
These two fig trees both stand open to
your need for some hospitality.
You are welcome inside either one.
Each tree has a ladder rope into
the Wastelands Maze if indeed your plan
is to continue onward, further east.
Might I surmise Horeb as your goal?
Kóre's eyes brightened at the name.
O quite right, dear sir! How did you know?
Yeoman saw hunched Simon flinch a bit
at the name of Horeb spoken so.
I can see the stains of coconut
upon your cloak. I know whom you have seen.
And too your feet are able to tread well
upon the green Peace-Stone, which means
you are being fit for Horeb's air.

108

Kóre felt a rush of joy rise up.
Very true, sir. And we are in flight
from the evil Queen who chases us
night and day without any reprieve,
and no doubt she'll soon pick up our trail.
That is why we forge ahead with haste
to finally find our refuge in the Cave
Elijah sent us seeking days ago.
Simon seemed to be more fidgety
as the subject of Queen Jezebel
entered into the earnest conversation.
Nathaniel pondered silently, then said:
Very well, then. Let us make it plain,
each of us, our tree and where both lead.
Simon and myself have different views
of the way to Horeb and our rooms
here in the high figs are suited each
to our frame of mind. We'll tell you how.
As if they had done this speech before,
Simon took his cue and toddled forward,
as if somewhat sheepishly it seemed
to Yeoman, watching carefully his ways.
He stood before his tree. Night was nearing
end and the dim light was able to reveal
the character of leaves that swaddled around
his tree. All were brown and withered as
if they had long been wanting water; or worse
perhaps some time in the past they had been cursed?
He cleared his throat and with his thin-pitched voice

made this case for staying in his tree:

I can see that you are very tired,
and well you should be after such travail.
Life was not meant for long toil and ail,
but for the fulfillment of desire!
Tell me: do you not ardently admire
that state of affairs of ease, where leisure's frail
atmosphere is safe from demand's assail,
where food and ale cheer, and by the fire
tiptoe in with sleep the sweetest dreams
with all the work behind? The sign of kings
is that they need not lift a finger should
they so choose. Is not their life the good
all of us would readily consent as best?
The life defined by freedom found in rest.

My Fig Tree is ease! An easy sell!
I admit it is a mess but then
I use magic to clean it up again
and I need never tend the work myself.
My time better spent, and for my health,
seeking ever new amusements when
the previous entertainment starts to thin.
I can conjure up an endless wealth
of new affections that require no urgent
effort. It is why once I desired
to have Holy Spirit's power to use
as I sought new ways to be amused.

Peter , kill-joy, said I did not aspire
to know Her, but only use Her as my servant.

All this talk of knowing God is burden!
It costs too much while never getting done.
Meanwhile, easy picking, chance for fun
are everywhere at bargain prices certain!
Nathan tells me that I'm impertinent,
but who is he to say? I'm the one
who knows for me my best! I've begun
a life of ease which I'm finding pure fun!
Though it's true I bore more easily
with a narrowed band of feeling's range.
Still the measure of my happiness
is the absence of all hated stress,
which is such relief, though I find it strange
my sleep is not as deep as it used to be.

Stay with me, and you will not mind the mess
as reckless mirth free-dances in your head.
My cupboards are well stocked with drink and bread.
And later when you leave you'll not need guess
the trail to guide you through the Wasteland test.
It is the shaded route, by shadow led
in the canyon bottom, trickle fed
beside an innocent brook affording rest
all along the way, where rarely sky's
oppressive blanket can be seen above,
such is the premiere quality of shade

taking all the weight of heat away
almost like a magic trick! You'll love
the bottom trail's ease on feet and eyes.

Simon all this time was mindless of
his over-animated pitch. He failed
to sense how hard he worked to make the case
that work was in all cases something bad.
Sweat had formed a ring around his head
like some friars of old, who beneath robes
harbored what was alien to their vows.
He stopped, expecting Kóre to leap up
into his open gesturing flabby arms
(even though, with the rapidly rising dawn,
the tree's appearance worsened with each tick)
so convinced he was his way was best.
Nathaniel, looking on, with folded arms,
smiled throughout, knowing that the smell
of sales pitch's artificial air
would be rank for one who had breathed real.
Kóre thanked him for his generous word,
then looked away to hear Nathaniel's part.
Simon sputtered incredulity
that the pair would even want to hear
another option laid out for their choice,
at which Nathan sat down on the ground,
leaning up against his tree, he spoke:

I must confess my fig tree home is sparse.
Little food I have, and little drink.
There are no beds to sleep on, and I think,
there are no blankets, save a couple coarse.
I am always hungry. It's the force
that drives my waking. I do not shrink
from working for I am always on the brink
of finally finding access to the source
of goodness everywhere manifesting.
My body longs for sweet fruit from this tree;
my soul thirsts for beauty's mystery;
my spirit yearns for God Himself to be
the voice I hear at night, the face I see
whether in the rest or time of testing.

Hear me, friends, and know there is a kind
of lingering want for truth that's sweet to bear.
It gives life its motion, steers it where
it most wants to go but cannot find
unaided. Desire unfulfilled in time
calls us through time toward the timeless where
true seeing is. Heeding the call is to stare
hard at everything the way a miner
aims to extract gold by persistent digging.
And there is no joy like joy when come
together two halves that surely belong
and have long been separated from
the other by time, or turn, or tacit wrong,
but at last are sewn into one rigging.

The work is seeking. Too, it's being sought.
The first is energy, the latter rest.
And this becomes the rhythm that is blessed,
like night and day. As any craft is wrought
by press and then release. By cold and hot.
Seeking is against unknown to press,
to feel, to risk, to tender careful guess.
To be sought is slowing until caught.
Both are the reunion. We are made
in a mold from which we long have strayed.
But never has the homing signal ceased,
calling us by robbing us of peace
until we cast off every substitute,
grafting to the singular first root.

From my barren house I'll let you down
on my ladder rope into the Maze
upon the trail that is safe to blaze,
the only trail safe in Wasteland ground.
A way of scarcity, for it runs upon
the tops of bluffs, exposed to full sun rays:
an austerity at odds with lazy.
Drive hard forward. Avoid the refuge found
in the shadowed canyons, for the rains
will come upon the land in a sudden rush
unleashing sheets in furious downpour flush.
The canyons will turn raging floods that claim
anything within their path alive.
These are torrents no one can survive.

114

With these words Nathaniel looked aside
at Simon who had slowly backed away
and without another word had slipped
up into his withered fig tree home
muttering all the while as he went.
Why is his tree shriveled like it is?
Kóre asked her curiosity piqued.
Nathan stroked his beard and soberly said:
He lives in the very tree the Master sought
a fruit once long ago and it was not
ready as it should have been and so
He cursed it to be as it meant to go.
It had withheld fruit; such its desire
became its destiny: its self its sire.
There was something tragic in the character
of Simon, for which Kóre felt a solemn sadness.
Looking up, her host had disappeared,
so Kóre followed Nathan up the tree,
Yeoman on her shoulder as they climbed.
The leaves were fresh, the vines easy to grab,
and many footholds in the trunk beside
made the ascent easy. Kóre felt
an increasing sense of hunger as she climbed
and upon reaching the high fig tree floor
where they were to sleep until the night
when they would begin the traverse of
the Wasteland Maze, she drew her jar of water
and drank generously only to find
the thirst deep in her throat resisted all

attempts at assuaging, but she found
even this carried a small pleasure,
a sign that Horeb's air was drawing nigh
and the water there that trickled cool
was even now quietly calling her name.

When early evening overtook by stealth
the slumbering afternoon dulled by heat,
Nathan shook his guests awake and bid
them to be upon the journey's way.
Travelling across the Wasteland Maze
was best done under night's cover because
they would need traverse exposed across
the bluff tops where in daytime birds of prey
circled over the canyons hunting victims
weakened by the relentless purge of sun.
Too the moonlight would in a better way
expose the dangerous cracks wide enough
that could swallow Kóre should she step
inadvertently into the gap.
For in daylight's heat the shimmering
above the ground could act as camouflage
and blend the cracks as if contoured ground.
But in the night the cracks looked black as scars
ripped across the tired desert flesh.
Nathan now gave last minute instruction:
Never once descend into the canyons,

even if some trails lead you down.
It is always, always dangerous ground,
for no one can know when the flash floods come.
The Way will be connected by old bridges
offering safe crossing bluff to bluff,
firmly anchored to the cliff-top ridges
even if they don't seem strong enough.
They will hold your combined weight alright.
They are called "faith-walks," flimsy to sight
but invisibly tethered side to side.

Yeoman flew up high to gain perspective
and sense of direction. He gasped to see
beyond the daunting Maze before him rise
up from the horizon, purple bathed,
and stretching to the clouds, as if on fire,
the majestic mountain, reigning on
the rim of the old world as if to bid
welcome to the humble pilgrim come,
and warning to all wise foes, stay away.
Horeb's sight to Yeoman was a jolt
of joy and inspiration. Like a stone
he dropped to Kóre's shoulder bearing news,
breathless in a most endearing way,
that before them lay their long-sought haven
in the clearest field of vision yet!
Only one more valley to traverse,
and though it be a trial, the mountain would
ever-increasingly claim more of their view

and turn the churning charming by and by
if they would keep looking up. And so
with warm embrace, Kóre bid their host
goodbye. Nathaniel put around her neck
a glowing jewel, a small translucent pearl.
Let this pearl remind you if should come
a moment you feel lost. It won't be true.
Though you won't know the way to turn,
all the while, He'll be watching you.
Listen closely: through the pearl He'll send
pulses. By their number on the dial
count and turn, as sun, your course to bend:
in so doing and in a small while
you will find the faith-walk bridge to cross,
keeping you from wandering off as lost.

Full of hope and joy and a day of rest,
water jar brim-full and angel cake
remaining, as was still some coconut,
feet flesh strong, and cool air in the lungs,
Kóre on the rope ladder step by step
dropped down to the flat top of a bluff,
towering above canyons on all sides.
Happening to look up as she went down,
she caught a final glimpse of Simon's face,
glaring at her from his withered tree,
mouthing something, muttering something bitter,

as what looked like shadows flew out from
his tree-top perch into the quiet night.
The moon was full and they, surveying the way,
saw all clearly made for what it was.
The intrepid pair set off to cross the Maze,
while dark vultures watched from high above
hidden in the black smudge spread of night.
The first part of the crossing was not hard.
Bluff by bluff they crossed the bridges each
which seemed sturdy enough and anchored well.
Looking down from mid-bridge they could see
the shadows of the canyons far below
seeming hungry like awakened bears
fresh from winter slumber. From below
were low and gravelly moans that sounded like
wind on old trees pushing, but not quite.
So their night passed never losing sense
of a restless hunger deep inside
driving them with focus ever forward.

The morning sun brought with it bolts of breeze
that quickly turned to whistling wind that turned
the dust into a million pronged assault
of sting and lash. Yeoman bravely spread
his wings to make a scarf for Kóre's face
and doubled over they tried to make their way.
Buffeted as they were, they were not sure
if they were headed as they should
as all sight and reference around

now were swallowed up in angry dust
and menacing brown. But then Kóre felt
the slightest set of pulses at her throat.
Looking down the pearl of Nathan glowed
when again three pulses gently throbbed.
Three shifts to the right! She turned and leaned
into the blustery row, but now she knew
she had a guide who from without
the storm could steer her true while she was in!
He Himself, the Horeb King, took interest
in the journey of a peasant girl and owl.
Oh what strength the thought of this infused
into her spirit despite the biting wind.
And it crossed her mind that Jezebel,
if by chance that she was somewhere near,
would not have such help, and thus the storm
which had only a moment past seemed grim
now appeared an ally in her quest
to make Horeb's shore ahead of her
evil pursuer, wherever now she was.
Eleven pulses now. And to the right
at that count in truth then steered her left
by a few degrees. And so it went
until they came to a faith-walk bridge that swung
wildly back and forth in the pounding wind.
It creaked and at the anchor point seemed worn.
Many of the footboards had been lost
and there were as many gaps as links.
The far end of the bridge could not be seen

through the squalling dust, no way to check
the state of anchoring on the further side.
No use Yeoman's wings in this strong storm
to traverse the gap for an inspection;
he could not compete to keep a course
and should he try who knows where he'd be blown.
The glowing pearl was still which meant that they
were on the right course. What did he say?
To trust each bridge no matter how it looked?
It was his word, and he had led them true.
Kóre took a breath underneath the wings
of Yeoman still wing-protecting her face
and stepped onto the madly swaying bridge.
She gripped the side wound ropes as tight as she could,
Yeoman's talons digging in her shoulder,
and placed one foot, then the other, at
each juncture where the rope rail looped into
the gangway in order to gain the smallest
measure of better hold. How hard it was
to even take a step! And after time
that seemed interminable, the pair had gone
only part way, clinched and hanging on
for life and limb and hope for the other side.
When suddenly the winds stopped in a snap!
The dust fell from the sky like falling flour
at a baker's bench. Nathan had said
the changes in the weather would be quick,
but this was unlike anything Kóre had ever
experienced before. Now that everything

was calm and clear, Kóre could clearly see
her predicament and almost then
wished for the return of the dust storm—
for sometimes seeing is harder than keeping blind.
She was on the longest bridge of all:
perhaps a mile to go to the other side.
Down below in the canyon, sight of sights:
Jezebel, surrounded by her dogs
and the chariot crew, were pointing up
at her. As they were still far below,
she could hear no words but echoes of
the barking dogs, more riled up than ever
by the storm and now by catching scent
of Kóre dangling from the rickety bridge.
Up above, in place of dust cloud, now
a swarm of angry vultures, weathered and mean,
were flying in formation with intent
to dive in squadrons at the exposed pair,
and flinch them off the bridge into the arms
of eager Jezebel below in wait!
How could they have converged all at this point?
How could Jezebel have found this canyon
at this moment and through such a storm?
What black magic aided their pursuit?
The thought of scorned Simon flashed upon
her mind and there she saw his final grin,
the flitting shadows then these very birds,
Simon plotting to have the last word still,
to force them into the canyon after all.

It was hard to even move without
losing balance and then tumbling over.
And now in waves the vultures were in dive,
sharp beaks swiping at the huddled pair,
and now dropping stones upon their heads!
One stone struck Kóre in the back
and knocked her breath full clear out of her lungs
but did not shake loose her desperate grip
on the dandling bridge under assault.

Suddenly a thunder rocked the air!
And just as fast the brightness turned to grey.
Not this time the dust but low rainclouds
roiled and writhed above the Wasteland Maze!
A swipe of lightning snapped across the sky
and with the next resounding drum of deep
and bellowing thunder fell the rain in sheets
pouring down as if they were underneath
a brand new river forging its fresh way
through the vales of sky instead of earth.
Pouring, pouring down, and Kóre found
relief from the bombing vultures, having fled
to find their cover back in Simon's tree.
Kóre raised her head and she could see
rushing down the canyon from the north
an avalanche of angry water on
the tear, tumbling through the canyon grooves
as if in a furious race to reach

the far end before other channels would.
White foam writhing at the stampede head,
brown in churn, and drag and swallowing
everything between the canyon walls.
Jezebel was busy looking up
at the swaying bridge, still thinking that
the rain would be her ally to bring down
drenched and tiring Kóre and her owl.
Not until the last, upon the sound
of a thousand thundering horses bearing on
her tiny company, did she then look
and only had a moment for a shriek
before the raging maelstrom overtook
her in a lightning strike and she was gone
and all her dogs, her chariot; all below
was muddy river pushing on with drive
unmerciful and oblivious of its prey.
The level of the flash flood kept on rising,
nearing now the top of the canyon walls,
and tearing at the bridge's anchor bolts
clinging ever so precariously
to the granite wall, until they broke
all at once! Kóre gave a shout
of sheer surprise and Yeoman, flung airborne,
immediately grabbed at the back of Kóre's
shirt to try and pull her out and up.
But the fabric tore and with the bridge
Kóre fell into the raging stream.
Clinging on was all she knew to do,

and good it was, for now the bridge, which seemed
a rickety affair when dangling high,
when in the water made a sure lifeline
with one end still fastened to the far wall.
The rush of the water pushed Kóre under,
and with both hands holding on to the bridge-rope,
she could not push herself to the surface
without being swept away for good!
But now her breath was about to run out,
and Yeoman was now useless in the wet,
his feathers soaked beyond any flapping good!
Just before Kóre was about
to give in and give up her lifeline hold,
a powerful buoyant force pushed her upward
despite the massive muscle of the water
rushing overhead. The buoyancy
was due to the pack upon her back, still strapped
securely there. But why would her drenched
pack, heavy with objects, float upon
the wild river? Kóre's muddled mind
could not understand the mystery,
but she was desperately glad once again
to gulp in precious air! She found if she
turned and faced the sky, the pack against
the water, she could easily keep her mouth
out of the danger of the water's reach,
and she could breathe and calm herself and keep
her concentration firmly on the task
of holding on to the bridge-rope for as long

as it would take for the flash flood to pass by.
The downpour now had ceased. The river raged
less and less until—when it seemed
she could hold on no longer— the water calmed
to where Kóre could simply hook her arm
on the rope and give her clenched hands a break.
The relative stability now gave Kóre
a chance to rest and to wonder why her pack
was floating like a life-boat, until Yeoman,
looking like a mounded pile of fur
with two orange eyes peering out despite,
suddenly cried out with sheer delight:
The comb of Absalom! Do you recall!
He told us should the time ever come
we should be overcome by rushing
water, the comb would keep us well afloat!
Ah, of course, sighed Kóre. *I was to wear*
it in my hair and still it worked its power
buried there within my carrying pack.
Is there no end to the mercy I
receive along this long and treacherous way?
Kóre now could clamber along the bridge,
riding atop the table of the flood.
Holding on both side-ropes life-line tight,
and Yeoman on her back, she made her way
in a kind of slow-motion drag and crawl
toward the farther side wall now in sight.
Pull by pull steady progress made,
slowly elevating toward the ridge,

Kóre now out of water climbing up,
up and up she made it to the top,
clambered out and on firm land again,
fell down beat, drenched in every part,
in every bone and muscle aching deep,
but safe having crossed the longest bridge!
The pearl necklace glowed as in applause.
Kóre laid awhile to regain
her strength. She sat up, and looked over the side
to see the once wild river receding fast.
Rainclouds gone and sunshine had returned.
No sign of Jezebel and her dogs
could be seen or heard. And as she turned
around she gasped to see how close now seemed
Horeb's towering rise looming large.
The way was level now and easy going.
There were bridges still but they were small
and they crossed them with a confidence
they had not before. Such is the way
of faith, where every smallest exercise
of it causes more mass to the muscle.
Maybe then the bridges only seemed
smaller but in fact were much the same
as some earlier daunting ones. But now
Horeb's rise remained before their eyes,
growing larger with each passing mile.
The air itself was laced with cool crisp strands
even though the sun was undiminished.
Along the path the shrubbery increased

127

from the occasional bush to crowded field.
And finally in this way they came up to
the final bridge of the Wasteland Maze and crossed
over into Horeb's lowland pastures,
where around in ever growing numbers
cattle grazed, and sheep beside them, herds
thickening with the slow ascending grade.
Here was Horeb now before them clear
and taking up well more than half of sky.
The top was blackened from the crown and down,
there where the old fire of God had fallen
in the day of Moses and the laws.
Mighty boulders scattered round the base
as if they'd once been blown out from within
the earth: the bowels of Horeb, monument
against any idols tainting sacred space.
Trees too had grown up in the lands
surrounding Horeb's feet like a garland thrown:
Tamarask and Terebinth and Palm,
Juniper and Sycamore and Fig,
all the trees that Kóre had come to know
and love by means of their salvation through
the Keepers that had led her along the way
to find this long sought-after mountain slope.

EIGHT

EVE,
KEEPER OF THE TREE OF POMEGRANATES

Winding higher now past boulder and tree,
Yeoman spending more time in the air
than on Kóre's shoulder, now dried out,
they came upon, by smell first, then by sight,
a tree that they had never encountered before,
heavy with sweet pomegranate fruit.
At this tree, as had so often been
the case at every tree junction before,
the trail split in two directions thence:
one off through the boulder field left,
the other hard right through a grove of trees.
Now Kóre knew that she should call
out for surely there would be above
in the thick lush foliage hidden well
a Keeper home, and one to tell them which
was the way to lead up to the place
of Elijah's Cave somewhere above.
Ho there! Keeper of the tree of fruit!
Are you there and can you help us out?
We are seekers for the way of truth
and need help to find our way about!
We are bound and have been for some time
for the whispering Cave on Horeb's heights.
Can you tell us whether left or right
will lead us faithfully where we seek to climb?
Suddenly a melody like a snake
uncoiled itself upon the evening air—
a haunting, beautiful song, effortless,

a language Kóre knew not, though could tell,
the song was invitation, but to what
was not clear at all. Then a sense
of something like a sleepiness set in,
as if a sorceress cast a drowsing spell,
but it was peaceful, full of pleasantness.
After such travail who could blame
the weary travelers from slanting toward sleep
at this bidding to lie down and rest?
Suddenly from above a woman spoke:
gentle was her voice and fine her face,
a beauty exquisite, the kind that's born
from innocence. With wide light blue eyes
and hair that flowed abundant around her shoulders,
falling down around her waist and so
for her it served as a cloak and what she wore
underneath could not be seen. She spoke
in a strange way, as if reading a script.
The look in her eyes did not line up well
with the substance of her memorized speech:

Choose, O travelers, in this very minute:
eat this ripened juicy pomegranate
filled with a deep-boned power to make you wise
enough to evolve beyond Elijah's Cave
and become fit for a cave of your own making
somewhere on this wide and beautiful slope
where you both are hereby free to go
anywhere you wish. Or, just say no

to this mystical fruit and remain dull,
in need of Elijah's Cave to make you full
but by gift from others and not yourself.
Choose, O travelers, now, and choose well.

The woman's eyes were burdened as if trying
to help them with their choice but she could not
speak a further word, but waited in silence
for Kóre to respond, whose simple wisdom
served her well, for thus her thinking went:
I have come so far and suffered much
to find Elijah's Cave, only to now
cast it off for a cave of my own making?
This does not add up, and even though
I must admit there is subtle appeal,
I fear this is a test I would be failing
to eat this fruit and fall into its offer.

Kóre spoke back to the woman clearly:
Thank you, most kind lady, for what you offer.
But we have eaten angel cake , and too,
coconut from great Deborah's palm.
Our thirst is managed well from this old jar
that never ceases to run out of water.
We are well and now need nothing more.
We will wait until we finally come
to Elijah's Cave and there to grandly feast.
I do not desire my own cave in the least.
In that moment the sleepy heaviness

in the air vanished like opening
the window of a hot and stuffy room
to let in cool outside air. The lady
laughed out loud and clapped her hands with joy,
and of a sudden fully seemed herself!

Welcome, Kóre! Welcome Yeoman too!
I have seen you coming now awhile.
For through every tree leaf I can see
and I have watched you across the long miles,
praying that you would know what to do
at the choice temptation of each tree.
Surely you have passed each test, and this
one too! How I hate to be the vessel
of the pomegranate fruit temptation.
But it is my fate to stand and offer
to all travelers what was offered me,
so I might know the grieving pain
behind the gift of freedom offered all.
I am Eve, the Keeper of the Tree
of Pomegranates, also known in fame
as the Tree of Knowing Good and Evil,
the fruit which I once took in covert bite,
holding juices of the knowledge of
light and dark, a knowing from within.
I forever tend this tree, and after
serving as the voice of fresh temptation,
for all who dare resist its Siren charge,
I am charged to then provide direction

to Elijah's Cave and serve as helper,
and all of this I do most gladly bear
as a testament of gratitude
 for my costly rescue by the One
who crushed the serpent's head by deep-bruised heel!
You are here in the lowlands, but beware:
two more tests ahead before you're there.
Do not let your guard down nor allow
even so to think that Jezebel
has perished in the flashfloods of the Maze.
She has life yet on this side of hell.
What she can survive is sure to amaze
even the most gullible but still
keep your focus, keep sharp your own will.
Enough now. Come and rest with me the night.
I will tell you now what path is right.
In the blink of an eye the duo found
themselves inside the Pomegranate Tree—
how they'd got there must have been a magic
from the early Eden days when all
was soaked with fresh power from the Word that birthed
the bright beginning and the wondrous rest—
resting on floor cushions comfortably
and ready now to hear which way to go.

Even here round Horeb's lowlands, there
rings a trail of idol soil laid
on this place ever since the day
Jacob's Children, having passed dry where

moments before had sprawled the Red Sea, snared
by old rebellion, chose to disobey.
After grace their lust of heart displayed
their deeper disposition, and they dared
build the Golden Calf and call it God.
This is what the lustful urge procures:
rejection of the present by crafted lures
of the appetite. It's very odd
how lust unhinges reason and drives passion
to steer the body into ruinous action.

The boulders left lead through to Mud Lust Way.
It starts out rocky and dry but in short time
will turn into a mud-path that will bind
to your feet and thicken quickly. Vain
will be shaking it off. Instead pain
of gradual sinking. You cannot climb
out of it. Lust throughout all time
has seduced the wary and the vain
by either appetite that's right for wrong
objects as its end, or other hand,
appetite awry for objects grand,
both spoilings rooted in the throng
of undisciplined impulses on a tear.
Either way the end is dark despair.

Lust's peculiar irony such is:
once it tastes its aim it will need more
of the thing to reach the previous floor

as the object's power diminishes.
In proportion to the rising wish
the actual fades away into a bore,
then to be discarded, searching for
what will fill the ever-increasing itch.
Discrimination of the finer things
will settle for things that just can be had.
And in the having never will be enough.
Raging thirst adrift on an ocean tug,
water everywhere but none to drink,
the wild-eyed sailor slowly going mad.

Lust begins with a restlessness in heart,
and some greener spot in easy reach.
The green is an illusion, time will teach,
but not until one's world is shred apart.
Often the first root desire is part
of the Pure First Longing. But as each
desire drifts away further out of reach
the Real-Turned-Idol's vicious power starts.
Do not even take one step upon
this Mud-Lust Way. Do not think you're strong
enough to withstand all its pulls and wiles.
Manageable may seem its many aisles,
but every one leads to the sucking mud,
which once it has you never will give up.

Even as Eve spoke Kóre could feel,
as she peered out from the Pomegranate Tree,

a definite tugging toward the Mud-Lust Way,
as if it were an exotic avenue,
a well-deserved indulgence after so
much stress and unremitting suffering.
She suddenly wanted to see around the bend,
to see exactly where the mud began,
wondering what the texture between her toes
would feel like? After all that very long while
treading on the green Peace-Stone…but then
Kóre looked at Eve who looked at her
with a piercing glance fierce and severe.
Though she uttered nothing, it was loud—
the warning rising up behind her eyes.
Kóre couldn't hold her gaze but broke
away and felt a flush of sudden shame.
After having come so far, how easy
it would be to follow strange desire
and bring an end to all the labor won.

The Pure Heart Path through the tree grove is not
actually a trail but a guided way
marked by traces of a moss, green-grey,
and in the light of day quite hard to spot.
The way will take you through a scree field wrought
with danger of rock-avalanche, save you stay
on those rocks on which the moss-marks lay.
And this for quite a length until it stops
at the edge of the Mud-Lust fields where lie
log after criss-crossed log of fallen trees

upon which you must balance all the time
to avoid the luring mud trap underneath,
the particular way mapped out by the line
of green-grey moss patches leading you by sight.

To find your way requires a single eye,
trained to recognize the green-grey moss
and tell it apart from other shades and blots,
and do so in real time. This focus, fine
and steady, hard to hold, comes about by
saying yes to paying the fixed-eye cost:
giving up the sight-seeing pleasure, the loss
of which to many is price set much too high.
It is the eye that heeds neither left nor right,
when sounds call out, or smells seduce the nose.
It is the eye that picks apart the shade,
the subtleties of variation knows,
and will not doubt, will step with all one's might
upon the marked spot, even though faintly made.

This eye will adjust to every level of light,
continue its discernment even when
the storm clouds block the sun by pull of wind,
or even in the thickest part of night.
What will happen over time, your sight
will learn to find the grey-green tint
even in the world of spirits, thin
as such is, invisible to the eye
of the untrained traveler on the land.

Soon what leads you won't be moss but hand
from the grey-green world pointing way,
and soon the guide will not be this, but He
Himself to Whom the way leads, His face made
out among the contours of the living grey-green.

Only such an eye can find the Cave
that you seek to find. All other eyes
when they pass it by will there surmise
it for a rabbit hole, or bit of shade.
On the long journey this far you have made
yourself ready for the single eye.
Now is time to let your old eyes die
and see in ways you've never seen! Be brave!
Eschew the Mud-Lust fields by focusing on
the set of clues upon the rocks and logs,
written in the life of the miracle moss.
All who seek will see and everyone
who chooses life, though daunting seems the odds,
will rise up high on Horeb's sacred rocks.

Being late and eyes desiring sleep,
Eve blew out the candles and in voice
nurturing bid the weary duo rest.
In the morning they would take the way
across the scree and to the maze of logs
following the trail of the moss.
Kóre noticed in the sudden dark
how along the walls inside the tree

an array of faint grey-green etchings
decorated the space with a peaceful glow.
Kóre's eyes were riveted on the patterns
as if her eyes had entered into training
for the next leg of the journey. Before
she knew it she had fallen fast asleep.

Yeoman woke up first and rustled round
the little room until Kóre too was roused.
Eve was nowhere to be found. A last
temptation: would they take her word?
Quickly to the right they started out,
toward the wooded grove and the scree beyond,
the Mud-Lust Way diametrically behind.
To the sloping hill covered in rocks
they headed resolutely with fair speed.
Looking up they could see, here, there,
little avalanches started by
slightest breeze, or a scurrying lizard's tail.
Treacherous would be this way, the footing false,
except for the marked stones, and now they looked
to see the sign of the green-grey moss spread out.
All the rocks were splotched, and shadows too
dappled rocks with shade, and it became
apparent the discerning of the moss
would not be a matter of casual glance.
Staring harder, looking for their entry

onto the scape of loose rock, Kóre pointed
to a smallish rock in the shadow of another,
but from out of the shade, a greenish tint,
a bare-glow, smoldering, subtly tucked away.
Kóre felt a tingle like she'd felt the night
before when staring at the Pomegranate Tree's
interior walls. The time had come to see!
Yeoman, beating wings, took shallow flight,
and Kóre holding to his talons, stepped
out from the grassy ground on which they'd
come to the edge of the perilous scree field
and onto the rock: it held without a budge!
She looked ahead, and there, a stride ahead,
another rock, not big, but plain to see,
matted with the moss and a tinge of green.
She stepped again, this time with quicker gait,
gaining confidence in eyeing the mark,
still with Yeoman fluttering overhead
to provide an airborne balance if
the rock should prove false and thus tumble out
underneath Kóre's landing foot.
Step by step they went in this slow way,
jump by careful jump. As the hours
passed in climbing higher, the pace increased.
The counterfeits appeared as such more
readily, and the grey-green moss became
more and more distinct as black on white,
or so the contrast began to seem to them.
Around them little avalanches spawned,

and once a stray rock from somewhere above
rocketed by and Yeoman seeing the flight
pulled Kóre to the right in time.
Up, then down, then up, then down again.
Never was there pattern to the route.
Only moss to mark the way and trust.
And trust proved trustworthy through the plodding day.
By evening they arrived at the scree field end
and came upon the fallen logs over grass
and mud just as Eve said they would find.
The light was dimming now, and Kóre mused
if they should wait to cross the logs next day.
But to their eyes, in dim light, moss-glow ramped
up a luminous intensity.
Kóre realized, just as in Eve's tree,
they would see the moss trail in the dark
even easier than they did in day.
They decided to press on. The dark
would obscure the tempting presence of mud
underneath the logs and mute lust's call.
Into night they ventured on the logs,
balancing at first with delicacy.
Kóre waving arms to straighten out,
and Yeoman always ready to leap up
into air to right the teetering girl.
Soon her feet proved sure and steady on
even thin and slippery shifting logs
as if she'd practiced on narrow beams or ropes
some time earlier in her yet young life.

She kept her eye upon the leading moss,
and trained herself to resist looking around,
for then her sense of balance would revert
to the sway and wobble. Once in late
night there sounded in the dark a cry
from some creature, loud and startling.
Kóre looked up on her instinct and
in that moment missed the next step on
the thin log she was crossing. Falling down,
she grabbed the log and slid right underneath,
wrapping legs around it in tight squeeze,
but dangling now above the lecherous mud.
Just how far the fall the darkness hid.
Yeoman hovered underneath her back
to give her push but the awkward angle blocked
the noble rescue attempt and still she hung,
unable to right herself, and then
from her backpack, shuffling in the hang,
tumbled out Elijah's precious jar
of renewing water and was lost
somewhere down in the evil sucking mud.
Kóre's arms began to shake and tire.
No amount of twisting could secure
reversing of this cursed capsized turn.
In this desperate state Nathaniel's pearl
that hung around her neck began to glow,
brighter and brighter like a fiery lamp
and lit the area up so she could see
more of what surrounded them in the dark.

Above the log to which she clung, a branch
jutting from another log nearby,
thick and strong, stretched out across the space
above them. Kóre whispered a command:
Yeoman, take the string that rings my pack,
the string that holds it closed, that opens it,
and pull it from its sleeve. Then sling it over
the branch that now above us we can see.
Kóre, breathing hard, laid out the plan:
Perhaps I can use it as a rope
to swing out from my log then back again
at a different angle from which then
I can scramble back upright again!
So Yeoman did exactly as she said.
His expert beak pulled out the pack flap string
(which then loosed the other goods in her pack—
the rest of the angel cakes and the coconut
and Absalom's priceless hair-comb gift, extra
clothes—all Kóre's possessions tumbled out)
and flew it up and around the Savior branch.
The two ends dangled within Kóre's reach.
She had to grab them both with one swift hand
(for to grab one end would pull it down!)
and bring her other hand to reinforce.
In a desperate swipe she let go of the log
and seized the two ends of the dangling string
with one hand, soon followed by the other,
and hanging for a moment to gain her bearing,
lifted and pushed hard with her feet and swung

out and away from the moss-marked log.
Then back into it, at her midriff bent,
just enough to leverage her shoulders over
the top, and with a clever kick of her legs,
catapulted to the topside safe,
and lay there breathing heavy and relieved,
heart still pounding at the narrow escape.
All because one distracted look away
at the sudden cry of a bird in the dark.
Kóre wondered if it had been the work
of one of Simon's deleterious vultures.
Sitting up she examined her empty pack
by the glow of the pearl around her neck.
It had survived so long, so far,
only to be useless near the end
with all the treasures from her newfound friends
lost to the quicksand mud below.
She fingered Nathan's pearl around her neck,
grateful more than ever for this gift.
She dropped the empty pack into the dark.
No more use for that, under her breath.
There was no time to let the sulk sink in.
To her shaky feet with new resolve
and with less weight, the balance even easier,
she trained her eyes upon the grey-green moss
leading her across the delicate patch-
work lay of logs, a net above
Lust's mud-fields, hungry for more drop.

Steady now, if slower, on they went,
Kóre concentrating like never before
until in time as if in a mirage
the glowing moss seemed to lift up off the logs
and hover above them like a coastline fog.
And soon the fog coalesced from fuzzy wisp
to thicker body, forming like a rope,
wending forward into dark ahead.
In time the long stretched rope form curled into
itself and became a single pillar
of radiating green cloud just ahead,
directing across the many cross-laying trees,
gentle, quiet, steady in its pace,
never rushing, never pushing on,
always as if invitation, easy
to follow. When they stopped to rest so it
would stop and wait like a patient guide.
And so it was in time that in the cloud
Kóre, if she wasn't looking straight
at it, from the corner of her eye,
could see a face with penetrating eyes,
full of love it seemed, but when she'd turn
to catch the countenance just cloud remained.
Until some moments later, having then
given up to see the face directly,
and looking through it to the way ahead,
the face again on the edges of her sight

would form, and Kóre even thought, with smile,
or maybe it was her mind-thought at play.
In this intimate, carefully guarded way,
through the night and into early morn,
Kóre made it safely to the end
of the network of slain trees over mud
and once again to solid ground beneath.
With the morning sun the green cloud vanished.
They found themselves upon a trail of stone
leading steeply up the mountain side
with deep brush and thorns on either hand.
It was clear which way was meant to go.
Up they travelled, steep step upon step,
breathing hard, and sweat on Kóre's brow.
Turning around the vistas of the land
were sweeping wide, and there across the valley
of the Wasteland Maze, with its bluffs and canyons,
on its furthest edge a blot—the Fig
Trees where Nathan and Simon held their watch;
and towering above that spot, cloud-ringed now,
on the far side of the desert stretch,
rose the mountain where stood Deborah's Palm.
Kóre even thought that she could see
the faintest spot where stood Saul's Tamarask,
or maybe this was imagination's add.
Higher still they climbed and thoughts of soon
coming on the Cave filled both their minds.
Now how far away could it still be?

NINE

JUDAS,
KEEPER OF HANGMAN'S EUCALYPTUS

———————————

Kóre felt the pangs of hunger driving
deep, and she had grown so thirsty that
now her tongue was sticking clumsily to
her mouth roof when she tried to speak to Yeoman.
They would both need water soon and food.
With this thought in mind they came up to
a mottled flaking Eucalyptus tree
standing in the middle of the path,
its peculiar russet bark conspicuous
against the backdrop of grey mountain cliffs.
From its lower branches—shocking sight!—
hung a bedraggled corpse, a weathered noose
around his neck. He smelled of death and rot,
and swung slightly in the mountain breeze.
Kóre approached cautiously. The smell
welled up nausea in her cramping gut.
On the other side of the protuberant tree,
two paths, as in past times, split each way.
Here another junction and a tree,
but the Keeper dead and who would speak
and give them counsel for the way ahead?
Pondering this conundrum, Kóre looked
and saw the flies buzzing around the head
of the bloated man. She took a stick
and waved them off: *respect now for the dead!*
she muttered at the flies.

                     None deserved,
the corpse answered back. His yellow eyes

opened upon the travelers who stood
below his dangling feet in fearful shock.
Do not be afraid, he hoarsely spoke.
I can do no harm now, nor wish any
more than I have already done. My name
is Judas. I am he, the hated traitor
that betrayed the glorious Innocent One.
Here my fate is sealed on this tree
of bleeding bark to expose the undercoat
true color and the mask of the hypocrite.
I hang here near the sacred Cave you seek
and serve to filter disingenuous pilgrims
who by feign and false front have somehow
managed to get this far and think success
is just around the corner—access to
the blessed Cave where dwells the Light and Life.
Sit awhile and I will tell you more.
Beside my tree there is a crumbling well.
Draw now up the bucket and do drink.
The water tastes of soil but is clean
and will brighten up your fading eyes
and give you strength to hear the words I speak.

Kóre, nearly faint with thirst, was in
no mood to be fastidious
and quickly found the well, and drew, and drank.
The water cold and mineral-rich revived
her flagging spirits. Yeoman drank some too.
They sat down upon the ground to hear

the wisdom Judas now knew, only wishing
he had known it earlier when it mattered.
In his coarse and gurgling hard-strained speech,
Judas told them of the final two paths,
only one of which led to the Cave.

To the right and through the berry leaves
lies the Glutton's Row, a dense, full way
where the power of appetite holds sway
and well-being is sought with every reach.
For at arm's length from any hand in sleeve
is the grasping of a ripe array
of the most delicious berries. Say
a kind and you will find it, each
and every one: blue and black and rasp,
cranberries, dewberries, strawberries, and the goose,
mulberries, barberries: like the Goblin plate
offered Laura long ago: a noose
around the neck of any who will grasp
them, gasping blue-faced. This, the glutton's fate.

Not so much in eating much, but eating
away pain and filling emptiness.
Finding hope by means of feeling less
empty in the moment, be it fleeting.
So the next bite furthers the unseating
of the gnaw, bite to bite. The rest
becomes an addict's sliding mess
into a pour, without end, always bleeding.

So close to the pleasures of the Cave,
the hillside Row of berries counterfeits
pleasure too with a robust tasty splurge
which, by the eating, submits to the next urge
as to the conqueror bows down the slave,
mastered by instead of mastering it.

The ways of berry eating, there are five:
hastily eating, gulping in a rush;
choosing only the largest of the bunch;
eating more than needed to stay alive;
frantic grabbing as if out of time;
or, picky in the look of what you touch.
All of these betray by giving so much
over to the power of appetite.
The bloating gut, the swelling from inside,
the vomiting, to return again and gorge,
dropping deeper into the berry breadth
toward the cliffs that these thick bushes hide,
until, heavy-lidded and body large,
heavy, one will fall to certain death.

To control the world by greedy grab,
to insure the future by locked store,
to insulate against the wave the shore
by walls of sand stacked high bag by bag
is the illusion cast to drive one mad.
As if Glutton's Row could ever lead toward
the security and sweet calm one for-

ever longs for, the longing long had
to be home. And there is only one
home to which we are fit to live,
like a key is shaped to only find
its match in one door and no other kind.
To that home the long wayfaring give
over to their rest, the searching done.

Judas now grew quiet. His strained speech
was a labor intense, not only to
deliver words, but relive his choice
to seek his home along the Glutton's Row.
Thirty pieces of silver was the prize
for which his clutching tumbled him over the edge
and to a death more horrible than can be
imagined, for the falling fell away
from the very gaze of Love itself.
Kóre felt compassion and whispered to
Yeoman to fly up, dab the tears that ringed
around the eyes of Judas, shut in thought.
To which kindness awakened him enough
to bear witness to the other way:

My strength fades me. Listen carefully now.
The other path, off to the left, there go!
It leads up to a rock-strewn harsh plateau
where upon its uneven jagged ground
through the ages have the old saints found
courage for their last stand, met their foe

and held unflinching against the fatal blow,
entering heaven with the martyr's crown.
The starkness of the place will be eerie.
The wind will howl, and shadows creep like smoke.
You will think you are there by mistake.
No, remember, this route you must take
if you are to pass beyond the cloak
that hides the Cave from eyes that cannot see.

I know now you're hungry. Such a spell
will you feel more upon the exposed height.
Your thirst will rage and daytime will feel night.
In your weakness gird up against hell:
prepare to encounter Queen Jezebel!
She hates Horeb but knows trails of blight
that come close to the Cave, yet out of sight.
She is raging, bound to catch you still.
No use turning back. Your trail's been traced
down there in the lowlands. Traps are set.
You cannot take Glutton Row. Please forget
that idea at once. No, you must face
your mortal enemy and you will find
a stranger blessing rising up behind.

Blessed are the persecuted few
ridiculed and mocked because they bear
the mark of the great king and proudly wear
his emblem on their forehead as you do,
given you the night you slept sleep true

in Elijah's Juniper, marked you there
as one who could drink the water without wear.
Marked you've been, as each Keeper knew,
and gave you guidance that has proven good.
And now you've come to me at last. The last
Keeper before the Cave to cast a light.
I know you fear her. Good, and so you should.
But God is fiercer, further up, and fast.
He will stand beside you in the fight.

With every insult that she hurls at you,
your wearying hunger will fade in clips away.
With every spitting spat and grimace made,
your thirst will disappear and strength renew.
With every blow upon your back, on cue
your courage will rise up with similar grade.
The more she strikes, the less she can invade.
Her every move on you will return two
blows upon herself and she will fall.
Not to say that you will not feel pain.
But pain a kind you've never known at all—
soaked in glory and solidarity
with Him who suffered torturous wound and shame
into resurrection. So will be.

Kóre's face had turned ghost white to think
that ahead lay one more time to face
the wicked Queen whose horrors she'd thought past.
Now to know a final showdown still

awaited her before the longed-for Cave.
Noticing her trembling hands, with care
Yeoman laid a wing upon her arms.
We have not come this far, my dear friend,
to falter now. As we have been, we'll be
carried on and carried through from here.
Kóre weakly smiled and knew it true,
though stubborn weakness in her knees remained.
Looking up at Judas, he looked down
through his pain and suffering, he smiled,
seeing in Kóre the determined eyes
that he had a time known in himself
but had faded at the berries' taste.
Wait till morning. Face her when the sun
is high above, for light will always be
your ally against such darkness as her.
And here— with this he dropped from in his cloak
a weathered bag that clanked upon the stone —
Take these silver coins, cursed as they are,
these that ruined my life, by them please ruin
the aspirations of the wicked Queen.
They are hardened through the long years since
I threw them down in horror on the steps
of the temple before His enemies.
Hardened now and sharp, but light to throw.
When the battle rages, use these coins:
throw them at the eyes of dogs and man.
Perhaps now they will serve a better end
and give me taste of that which could have been.

Thanking Judas, who had closed his eyes,
wearied beyond weary by his speech,
Kóre and Yeoman settled by the well
and curled up to pass the long cool night.
The wind had picked up ominously in the sky,
and Judas silhouetted against the rose
and orange of the sunset rocking back
and forth, made the peace unsettled such
that Kóre drifted into uneasy sleep,
nightmares racing through her restless mind.
Yeoman covered her, his look concerned.
The morning light was longed for and was not.
Sinister bearings hailed with the dawn.
And when it came, it came cold, like an old
coat left out and forgotten on the ground.

The sky was sterile-light before the sun
was even near its coming up and out
from under the blanket of the gloomy stars.
Yeoman woke. Kóre wasn't where
she had lain down in the night. A rush
of air and he was high and scouting her,
a fear of foul play, knowing foul was near.
But she was kneeling under a Juniper,
her eyes clenched tight, unconsciously fingering
the stone that Nathan laid round her neck,

praying, Yeoman saw, and drew near softly,
wanting neither to distract nor remain
outside the sacred moment under way.
Kóre opened up her eyes and smiled
at the sight of her most faithful friend.
I have asked if such a trial as we
have now come to expect might pass us by.
We shall see the answer in the going.
As it stands, I am prepared to die.
For even if I do the Cave is near
and perhaps my corpse might find its cool
air sufficient to return my life.
What I know is I will not be taken
as a captive nor will I return
to the lowlands with a breath in me
should the evil Queen advantage take.
And I with you, my Lady! Yeoman vowed.
Now to death, or to the overcoming
for which we've dreamt, and now must pass from dream
and into blood and stone to make our stand.

With the words and in the trembling tone
of heroes through the ages, Kóre set
upward toward the hill brim now ablaze
in morning wash of sunlight, thick like oil
oozing from the crevices of cloud.
Weak from hunger, no thought of the berries
beckoned, such the force of Jezebel's
imminent appearance marshalled all

energy into a focus she'd never known.
Now upon the rim she scoured the sweep
of the stony plateau on which she stood.
The ground was rough with sharp-edged rock spread out
embedded firm, not loose. Unmerciful
would such terrain be to any who fell down.
The narrow plateau was void of any trees
but ringed around by a wide variety,
almost as if this were a coliseum
like that of Ancient Rome where wild beasts
toyed with saints too worthy for the world,
holy ground where Perpetua unafraid
guided the trembling hand of her own slayer.
 Yeoman rode the currents above in wide
circles, sure to gain first sight and thus first plan.
Nothing stirred in the early morning hour.
The stillness was unnatural and cold.
Then a bark! Quite distant. But distinct.
The bark rode the breeze ahead of its
sender, spilling an early bitterness.
The vicious sound drained the color from her face.
Kóre searched to find a perch where she
would take her stand and wait the coming party.
Barking now in tumble growing thick
and from within its cloud the dreaded voice:
Onward, pets, devour her scent and bring
me to her for my sweet devouring!

There in the middle of the rock theater

sat a giant boulder looking like a head
of granite rising from a buried heap.
The face was shadowed where two eyes would be
and seemed to beckon Kóre come and stand
upon its head, for it was high and wide,
and certain the slick sides would fend off dogs,
and Jezebel would not have easy way
to gain a grasp of Kóre on the rock.
The boulder was not easy then to scale
but holes just right and laid out as if made
for the reach of Kóre made a kind
of hurried hewn-out ladder and what with
Yeoman with his talons at her back
and flapping wildly to aid her in the lift,
Kóre scrambled to the top in time
before Jezebel and her depleted
crew overtook the bluff's far crest
and rumbled rag-tag onto the plateau.
Still her chariot ran, ramshackled as
it was, pulled by two black horses with
the reddest eyes (Kóre was not sure
these were horses of the earth by look
and smell and snort). With her now were only
two men left and these looked crazed and worn,
draggling on along with vacant stare
and every other step a stumbling,
holding on to two dogs that were left,
snarling with the anger she had seen
before but now through rib cages pressing out

as if in rebellion, pressing to leave
the bodies of the beasts that bore them ill.
And Jezebel herself was tattered splay,
every hint of regal wrecked and ripped.
Even on her head the golden crown
always nesting on immaculate head
was simply gone (perhaps in the flash flood;
how had she even survived that wash?).
All that yet remained unchanged of her
were the steely grey eyes filled with hate,
filled with more hate now, more piercing mean,
piercing through to Kóre when their eyes
finally met after all this long, cruel chase.
The meeting was a fleet of daggered ice
flung into the chambers of her mind
with paralyzing stun. Kóre shook
her head and swore to avoid those eyes if she
could help it. And so there she stood upon
the outcropped boulder, Yeoman shouldered by.
Around her rope belt hung the silver coins.
Two she fingered, one in each taut hand.
Around her neck the stone of Nathan pulsed.
Firm she stood her ground and strong she looked
even though inside her heart bucked high
and she was losing feeling in her feet.
The evil rabble pulled up near the stone.
The Queen looked up without a word. Then smiled.
Well now, what have we here all surrounded?
I think what I've lost I've finally found.

It has been a trouble, but no trouble such
that I cannot get recompense enough.
And so I shall! Seize her! First the dogs
leapt upon the boulder sides and slid
down again upon each furious leap,
foaming at their mouths in delirious rage
but all to no avail. Scurrying around
all sides of the boulder, finding no
crevice upon which to climb up the face,
and finally turning back beside the wheels
of the chariot in which Jezebel
grimaced and contorted at their botch.
To her men she then commanded: *Go!*
They set out to clamber up the sides.
Being larger heavier men, the holds
held not hope for them to grab ahold,
slipping down each time they looked as if
they had actually begun a real ascent.
After a time, in which, if Kóre could
have watched this from afar she would have been
doubled over in laughter at the sight
of all the futile awkward climbing attempts,
the weary soldiers wearier were and sat
down upon the ground to take her venom
spewing now at their inept crusade.
Ag! Must I do everything by myself?
And with that ominous word Jezebel,
witch of evil that she was, began
to chant and fingered furiously the gold

medallion that hung around her neck
and which her lips had kissed a thousand times
in mindless full devotion to the demon
gods to which she'd yielded long ago.
Jezebel seemed lost inside a trance
until the smallest crook at the edge of her mouth
belied a smile as she then began
to levitate above the chariot bar.
Slowly, steadily, by the wicked charm
enabling her to walk upon the air,
Jezebel floated up and to
the far edge of the boulder and set her bare
feet upon the flat and stood now face
to face with Kóre, her fortress fully thwarted.
From underneath her soiled cloak she took
a rope that she uncoiled in threatening slow
manner never taking her eyes off
of Kóre standing poised, unmoved, afraid.
An acrid smoke ring seemed to waft
off the rope each time its lengths were dropped.
Strange it was, and stranger when, in flash
of an eye, she flung the rope up high,
and in the air it formed a ring and flew
over Kóre's head and around her arms
before she even knew, such was its speed.
The Queen snapped the rope tight and it squeezed
just below Kóre's shoulders and cinched
tight and immediately began to burn.
Kóre cried out in surprising pain.

Yeoman, flung aloft at the falling rope,
from the air grabbed the rope in beak
and too felt the immediate poisonous burn
and could not hold on though all his might
aimed again and again to break the hold.
Laughing now, Jezebel began to pull
Kóre toward her, caught in the acid rope,
branding her with the Jezebelian stripe—
the mark which circled everything she owned.
One step closer now to Jezebel.
Pushing back against the pull became
more excruciating. Kóre's head
began to swim with fear and pain in churn.
She felt the two coins in her hands and prayed.
Able now to move her tortured arms
at the elbow only, this she knew
that she would have one chance, the chance was small.
Could she fling the coins with enough torque
and sufficient aim to blind the Queen?
Wait, she thought, *a little closer yet...*
The smell of rotting flesh infused the air.
From below the dogs deliriously yelped
in eager anticipation of the catch.
Kóre felt the world begin to fade—
now or never! Then with all her might
coiling her shoulders hard (at what a price!),
she whipped her arm at the elbow like a sling
and flung a coin of silver toward the face
of gloating Jezebel, who as if on cue,

widened her eyes to see some object flung.
And right behind it from her left hand too,
Kóre flung the second coin with everything
she had left and fainted at the pain.

She never saw what happened. Yeoman would
later tell her how the two cursed coins
like two arrows from an expert's bow
found the saucered eyes of Jezebel
and sank into her sockets like fire through ice,
like rocks flung through a window, piercing deep
into the inner chambers of her brain,
lodging there and radiating full
the Betrayal of Ages in sour crash.
Jezebel screamed once a tortured *NO!*
And then collapsing backwards fell upon
her unyielding chariot, crumpling to
the ground, whereupon her dogs in sudden turn,
famished as they were through such long gruel,
leapt upon her body in ravenous feast
and picked her flesh clean, then turned toward the men,
who aghast and now without protection,
hunters now turned hunted ran away,
crazed dogs howling after them in tear
and surely caught them, if not they before
had found a cliff to lend them merciful death.
As soon as Jezebel fell from the rock
the rope that circled Kóre vanished up
into a mist and the breeze disbanded it.

Yeoman tried to rouse Kóre awake.
But she was still and cold. Her burns were raw.
Yeoman could not lift her off the rock.
What was he to do? The glowing pearl
around Kóre's neck was pulsing fast.
He remembered how the pearl had been
faithful guide when lost in the Mazeland storms.
Could the pearl now lead him to the Cave?
Certainly help would there be found and near!
In his beak he took the necklace pearl
and to the air. The pulses slowed, became
deliberate, the way they'd been before,
pounding out direction left and right
according to the sun dial's face design.
Looking only at the pearl, he flew
matching pulses with his darting aim
and soon felt more as if he was being pulled
than following a code. Until the pearl
stopped its pulse, extinguished all its glow,
and Yeoman stopped and hovering in mid-air,
before him, in the high precipice of
Horeb's darkened crown, between two sheer
cliffs — a beautiful tree, lavished with
fruit of many colors and many kinds,
heavy laden but in a happy way,
and there behind the tree, an opening!
Could it be the Cave? And suddenly
above the tree appeared a brilliant angel
emanating light but still with form

(a form that cannot be expressed in words)
swinging in his hands a mighty sword
in a continual circle cutting off
any chance of safely coming near
any branch of the tree alive with life.

TEN:

KÓRE,
THE LONELY CYPRESS KEEPER

———————————————

Help us, Sir, if you be friend of God!
Kóre lies nearby and nearing death
with the poisonous brand of Jezebel
burned into her body, yet she will
not belong to her in life or death!
With the coins of Judas she overcame
the evil Queen who has long pursued
us as we have long been pursuing you,
if this is the Cave I think it is!

The mighty angel stopped his swinging sword.
Hail, mighty warrior, Eagle-Owl!
You are right to see what you now see.
And there has never been a moment when
you and Kóre have not been utterly seen.
Come and rest upon the branches of
the Tree of Life. And do not worry so,
Kóre is already here and in
the care of healing angels who will turn
her suffering to balm and then into
medicine for others along the way.
But that is for another day. Now come.
There is someone who awaits you now.

Yeoman followed the angel as he sank
into the Tree of Life from the very top
as if dipping down into a pool.

Inside the wondrous tree, full of space,
were broad limbs easily bearing among the leaves
large fruits, radiant in scent and color,
pulp and juices ready to break free,
eager to be eaten. *These are for,*
quietly spoke the angel, *healing for*
the wounds of all the nations, the wounds since Eve's
scars birthing Seth, since Adam's sweat,
your wounds, Yeoman, and the burn of Kóre,
stored up here and waiting for the day
when the floodgates fall and reclamation
of the furthest things to near begins
the final culmination. So will be
the old passing to new and the end of tears.
The angel entered into a cavernous hole
in the side of the massive trunk and bid
Yeoman followed and to his surprise
heard the warm familiar greeting of
Elijah whom they'd met back at the start!
Welcome friend! I applaud your brave arrival.
It is now the twentieth day since you
and Kóre set out fresh from Raven's Crossing.
Cheerio! You made the journey in half
the time it took me. But I had no owl!
At each tree you wisely chose and found
the difficult path to Horeb. Difficult,
but not as difficult as would have been
should at any juncture you'd chosen other.
We are in the Tree of Life which once

174

stood in Eden's Garden. Ever since
the angel around its limbs has swung his sword
to bar access to those who would seek
its life to only perpetuate brokenness.
This Tree is for new and different life.
And in its shade and by the juice-strength of
its varied fruits you will find the work
of the Cave as a light and easy road!

Elijah, cheerful as always, motioned for
Yeoman to follow him through a tunnel maze.
In and out through the many Tree corridors
they made their way until a little room,
inside a bed, and Kóre sleeping there,
peaceful rest like Yeoman had not seen
since Birch Meadow days. *You may take*
your vigil here, dear Yeoman. I must make
for the Juniper of my keeping. There
are travelers soon due of whom I must guide
as I guided you. For now farewell!
And bid Kóre all the goodwill of
my heart. With that he vanished at a blink.

Kóre slept for several days. When she
awoke, she found Yeoman bedside who
told her everything that had been done,
starting with fall of Jezebel.
Kóre marveled to herself — the gift
of finally being here, the gifts

that she had known at every turn,
the gift that was her life, all of its parts,
even the horrid turn but that had served
to bring her here, and now an unimagined
future calling out. Once out of bed
the two explored the Tree through passages
winding like a labyrinth up and down,
tasting fruit with freedom, never full
and never hungry. They came upon a bridge
leading from the Tree into the Cave
into which they entered breathlessly.
Dark at the mouth, but once inside
all was light, not garish bright, but clear,
everything distinct and well-defined.
The Cave walls painted the story of the world
in amazing detail. They even found
the saga of their journey on one wall.
A river ran through the middle of the Cave
buttressed well on either side by branches
heavy with the fruit from the Tree of Life.
On the river moored were balsa rafts,
and into one Kóre and Yeoman climbed.
By the current they were carried deeper
in, breathing most refreshing air upon which
a cradling mist seemed to hover around them
whispering welcome, whispering welcome home,
whispering an encouragement to come
deeper in where nothing was forbidden
to the touch or sight. And so they drifted

on the river current for awhile.
At first alone, then they began to see
people everywhere, in purposes
intent but not yet clear, but full of grace,
busy bearing fruit this way and that.
People laughing the kind that comes from joy.
The river carried Kóre next into
a low-ceiling chamber with walls aglow
with a greenish hue: the Peace-Stone path
that had led her across the desert floor
was built with rock hewn from this mountain mine!
The mist around them took on different hue,
a lustrous green-grey hanging over the moss-
covered rocks along the river, and again
Kóre recognized it as the very
guiding force that had taken her through the scree
and across the treacherous logs. Again
it seemed as if from the corner of her eye
in the curling mist a smiling face
would hold a moment and then dissipate.
Through this chamber and into one yet
smaller Kóre floated until a stone wall
across the river stopped her raft in time—
just beyond it the river gave way to
a waterfall that fed a deep abyss,
pouring into the center of the world
it seemed to her. And then upon the wall
a man was standing extending out his hand.
Kóre took it and was pulled into

His arms and held in an embrace that wiped away
all the terror, all the lingering pain
of her long ordeal (though not by
erasing it from memory but by seeing
all of it from the vantage point of the
Love that was then pouring over her).
She looked up into the face, the face
that had looked upon her through the cloud,
the face she'd seen in troubled dreams at night,
the faint face in the shade of the Bogland reeds,
the face in the foam of the flash flood's rushing rage,
a face that looked almost like her father's,
a face she'd felt as if she'd always known,
and thought to ask a question, but to mind
no question came. Only desire to love
back if somehow she could find the strength.
And so you will, my Love, was all he said.

Her very next blink Kóre was standing on
the boulder upon which she had stood firm
and faced the evil Queen (such instantaneous
transport would take a little getting used to).
There was no shuddering to have now returned
to the place where she'd almost lost her life.
Instead she felt an elation rising up.
And there in the crack of the rock was rising up
a sprig of a tree, already grown a foot.

Beside her was the angel with the sword.
Dear Kóre, from your courageous stand
a seed fell from your sacrifice into
the crevice of this rock that once was called
Golgotha but now is known as Crown.
This little sprig is a Mountain Cypress Tree.
It will stand here as a sentinel for
all the pilgrims who must face before
their road is finished their own Jezebel.
So it is that all who seek the Cave
must stand up to what has long chased them
across the deserts of their worried world.
And they will need a Keeper's voice to aid
them in the choice to stand. And you are she:
Kóre with the courage of an owl,
Keeper of the Lonely Cypress Tree.
This will be your service to the King,
aided by brave Yeoman, if he choose
to take up a Cypress home with you!
(To which, of course, in Yeoman's owlish way,
his chest feather's plumed outward in pride).
The Cave is open to you; any blink
of eye will bring you there and bring you back.
To which Kóre kneeled on the rock,
bent down low above the tender sprig,
cradling it in her hands, she whispered low:
Grow, home, grow and send your roots down deeper,
so says Kóre, the Lonely Cypress Keeper.